RAILROADED

A Novel

JAYNE M. WESLER

Copyright © 2020 Jayne M. Wesler
All Rights Reserved.

Cover design by arshgrfx

First Printing: November 2021

Milford, PA

Saint Cloud, FL

ISBN 978-1-7355405-8-0

Published by Phoenix Consultation & Advocacy LLC

Jayne M. Wesler, Esq., LCSW

www.jaynewesler.com

This book is dedicated to my mother,
Betty L. Theime.

You are the quiet, shining light, and the gentle,
powerful force of love.

Acknowledgments

Special thanks to Vincent Czyz for his editorial guidance, which has certainly made this a better read.

TABLE OF CONTENTS

Chapter One

Whaaanhh whanh waaaanh! sounded the locomotive as it headed south out of the station. It quickly picked up speed as it shot through the night, wheels clattering as the wind rushed past.

Out of the darkness, a shape emerged, hurtling toward the speeding locomotive. A cry went up in the cold night air, but the engineer saw nothing until a figure suddenly materialized on the tracks.

No no no no! his brain shrieked as he reached for the emergency brake. *Too late too late too late!* He felt the impact, a hard *whoomph*. The brakes screeched as the train skidded and slowed until, the engine shuddered to a stop.

Officer Chris Brandt's radio crackled to life.

"10-56," said the dispatcher. "Jefferson Avenue and the railroad tracks."

"Jesus Christ, not another one!" Brandt hissed.

Ten-fifty-six was the code for suicide. Hitting the

switch for the light bar, Officer Brandt stomped on the accelerator.

During the 92 seconds it took him to race to the scene, memories of other recent suicides filled his vision. The body of an 18-year-old student who'd had a fight with his girlfriend, the girlfriend hysterical, weeping at the edge of the tracks. The teenager who, despite being a star athlete and top student, had felt so imperfect that suicide had been the impulsive solution to his misery. The brother of a young soldier who had been killed in the war, jumping onto the tracks because he felt guilty for surviving his brave older sibling.

Brandt pulled up to the empty railroad crossing. He could see the train stopped about 800 feet south of the crossing, steam hissing and rising from the engine. People were scattered on the tracks, a few in uniform who were obviously the train crew, and several others in various states of dress, including a hysterical woman in a bathrobe and slippers.

Striding down the tracks toward the front of the train, Brandt shone his police-issue flashlight along the gravel mounded under the tracks. There, a grisly sight made him falter: a sneaker-clad foot, severed and flung by the force of the train, appeared in his path. He squatted down for a closer look, then straightened and closed the distance to the engine and the crowd of people. As he approached, a crew member hurried toward him.

"Officer, am I glad to see you." The man extended his hand. "Joe Richardson. I'm the engineer on this run. It looks like a teenage boy or a young man is dead over there." Joe gestured toward the front of the train. "I saw him jump in front of the train. He just came out of nowhere." Joe was gesticulating wildly now. "I tried to stop the train, but we were up to full speed. There was just no way." Joe put his head down for a second in an attempt to gain his composure, then back up at Officer Brandt. "He looked right up into my eyes. He was screaming. There was nothing I could do."

"I'm sure you're right, Mr. Richardson." Officer Brandt gave Joe's shoulder a squeeze. "Now, I'm gonna need your help here for a moment until my backup gets here. Can your men keep the neighbors from contaminating the scene? They should have the onlookers back off the tracks and away from the entire railroad easement. They also need to be careful where they step." Officer Brandt waved his flashlight back the way he had come. "There's a foot down there."

Richardson stared for a moment. "Sure, sure."

It took a few moments, but the crew got the crowd—which had grown exponentially in the few minutes the train sat still on the tracks—to back off. Officer Brandt quickly cordoned off the area with yellow police tape, keeping the scene free from contamination but also giving some dignity to the suicide.

Officer Brandt then located the torso and the head of the dead boy, which were miraculously still intact, including the limbs on the right side of his body. As he knelt down to shine his flashlight into the boy's face, the sightless eyes looked back up at him. Officer Brandt felt his heart wrench. He sighed. "You poor kid. It's all over now."

It was well after 2:00 a.m. before Officer Brandt finished his shift—two hours later than usual. His heart was as heavy as his step as he clocked out and left the police department; he'd just finished cleaning up after a kid named Stan, who, at the age of 17, hadn't believed he had enough to live for. This case was weighing on him because it wasn't just a case: it was a kid. And not the first one, God knew.

There had been a rash of suicides in the past several years. Many of them opting for death by train. It was dramatic, effective, and a very public way to deliver the final Fuck You. A way to tell those who've pissed you off just how angry you are.

But it's so stupid! Chris thought. As a police officer, he was always around to see the aftermath. He sometimes had to notify the next of kin, which, in all of these cases, had been the teens' parents.

His mind flashed back to another train wreck two years earlier. That one hadn't been a deliberate death.

Did that make it better or worse? Chris wasn't sure, but he knew the horror of that evening still, deep in his gut, in his psyche. He'd been nearby when the call had come in—so close that he'd heard the train's emergency whistle, a repeated long-short blast combo, following by the screech of metal on a balmy October evening.

When he had arrived at the railroad crossing, what was left of the Nissan Pathfinder had been virtually unidentifiable. Steam rose from the car's engine, or what was left of it. The metal hulk was flattened around the front of a North Jersey Coast Line southbound train. Chris had rushed to the vehicle, where he had found two occupants, a female driver and a young male passenger. The passenger was deceased, his left eye blank and staring, the right side of his head reduced to gore from the impact. The woman was still breathing, though her pulse was thready and accelerated. She survived her initial surgery but never regained consciousness and died weeks later.

Shaking his head to rid himself of these memories, Chris unlocked his front door and went inside to shower, then to a hoped-for oblivion in dreamless sleep.

Chapter Two

Earlier that Sunday in late October, another local teenager had spent a typical day. Will Van Dalen was a senior at Ocean Beach High School, where he was captain of the basketball team as well as its star player. Tall and lanky with an air of coiled energy and a ready grin, Will also had sandy brown hair and blue eyes that were the subject of many a schoolgirl crush. A gifted athlete, Will had lettered in varsity basketball and varsity baseball. Despite his age—at 18, he was already an adult in the eyes of the law—Will was really still a kid: guileless, good-natured, and playful, kind of like a Labrador Retriever. Although he served as a decorated guard on his high school basketball team, he was, in reality, unguarded. He only got into mischief, not bad trouble, which is the irony that makes the rest of what happened to Will Van Dalen all the more unbelievable.

Will's home town, Ocean Beach, was a New Jersey enclave with a small, year-round population. Between Memorial Day and Labor Day, though, the population swelled with tourists. Throngs of vacationers and day-trippers flocked to the Jersey Shore to lie in the sun and listen to the laughing gulls call. Given its prolific sun and surf, the Jersey Shore had a long-standing reputation for restoring health and vitality. The miles of sand and surf at the Jersey Shore offered rest, relaxation, and recreation; the boardwalk and nearby eateries offered games, shopping, nightlife, and the delectable enticements of fries, burgers, ice cream, cheesesteaks, and fried seafood.

During the school year, though, the Bennys—the summer tourists who crowded and trashed the seashore area—had all gone home and left a certain woebegone air to the beach town. The nickname could be traced back to the train stations along the North Jersey Coast Line—(B)ayonne, (E)lizabeth, (N)ewark, (N)ew (Y)ork—from which these visitors emanated. With the exception of the tourism-dependent business owners, the locals enjoyed this quieter time of year.

For Will, his day at the shore had started off with chores: helping his father clean the gutters and rake leaves. Early in the afternoon, he'd helped his dad do the weekly grocery shopping. After all, it was just the two of them now. Will and his dad were close; they even looked alike. At six feet, two inches tall, Bill Van Dalen was fit and trim, still handsome at forty-eight.

Will had always been a good kid, but he was

often impulsive, restless, forgetful, and failed to pay attention—classic symptoms of attention-deficit/hyperactivity disorder. He was a dreamer who made careless mistakes—also symptoms of ADHD—but he was loveable, and he tried hard.

That October evening, Will was relaxing in front of the game on TV when he got a text message. He grabbed his keys, called good-bye to his dad, and headed out the door.

Chapter Three

Earlier on the evening of Stan's suicide, Will's six-year-old Kia Optima pulled up to the curb in front of the small, dilapidated winter rental where Troy Braithwaite lived with his father and his older brother, Marc. His mother had run off years ago in search of a better life, which had included exactly none of the men of the family. They all pretended she had died. Troy's dad drank to anesthetize his misery. Marc, who was 19, delivered pizzas by night and attended community college by day. Sixteen-year-old Troy, cleverer than both and twice as careless, figured he wouldn't break his ass to make money. If his father didn't care about him, he figured he'd better learn to pay his own bills. Someday he would kick off the dust of this little seaside town, which was pretty dead for most of the year, and head to the Big Apple. Then he'd make all his dreams come true. In the meantime, he sold dime bags on the side. He'd keep his head down, be his own enforcer, keep his seller happy, and everything would be fine.

Will and Troy had met two years earlier in the local hospital. It was Will's mother, Carolyn, who'd been driving the Nissan Pathfinder that had ended up wrapped around a North Jersey Coast Line engine. His little brother, Patrick, had died at the scene. They had been on their way to pick up Will from basketball practice. A sophomore at the time, Will had been insistent on going to practice every day. He was trying to make the varsity team, and nothing would keep him from practice—not even the family's busy schedule. Will slept, ate, and dreamt basketball. He was in love, obsessed. He had pleaded with his mother that morning for a ride home.

"Can't you walk home, just this once?" she'd asked, exasperated. Carolyn Van Dalen had been overextended that fall. She had gone back to school to become a nurse and was in the middle of the cardiac curriculum, a notoriously difficult section of the nursing program. Will's dad was struggling at the time with the long hours he had to put into his business, a lumber and landscaping shop in downtown Ocean Beach. Competing with the big boys of Home Depot and Lowe's had been much more intimidating than he'd expected. He was frazzled and so distracted by his constant worry that he barely knew what was going on at home.

In answer to Carolyn's suggestion that he walk home, Will complained that he'd be tired after a full day at school, an after-school workout with the team, then practice on top of that. Ultimately, Carolyn had given in to Will's pleas.

Even though the evidence showed Carolyn had shot the gate, making an impulsive decision that would be her last, Will was overcome with guilt. He'd beaten himself up with *if only, if only*. He'd kept a daily vigil at her bedside and stayed as long as the staff would let him. Sometimes they'd make him go home to shower and sleep, telling him that she needed some quiet. They'd really done it for Will, not for his mother. Most of them had heard him sobbing in her room at nighttime, begging her not to leave and apologizing for being so selfish and lazy.

One day during those interminable three weeks, Will was in the waiting room when he recognized Troy from the neighborhood. Troy was playing it cool while waiting to hear how his father's surgery had gone. Mr. Braithwaite's appendix had burst during one of his alcoholic blackouts and he'd ended up with peritonitis. His condition was listed as "guarded."

Since Troy was an eighth-grader and Will a sophomore, Will should have ignored him. It just wasn't cool to mix with a middle schooler, but Troy looked as lost as Will himself felt. Focusing on Troy helped distract him from the stunning void left by his brother's sudden death and his mother's critical condition, so Will invited Troy out for a slice of pizza. Will explained that his mom was likely going to die, despite the surgery. Only Will's father staunchly refused to believe it. But Will had absorbed the gentle information relayed by the doctors that his mother was fighting for her life. Her brain was swollen and they had opened a section of her skull to reduce the pressure. She'd also been bleeding internally—the force of the impact had torn a hole in her aortic artery. The surgical team had repaired it, but she had lost a lot of blood. The lead surgeon had ordered that Carolyn be put in a coma to allow her brain to heal, but by the end of the third week, even Will could see that she was deteriorating. During their pizza dinner, Troy had opened up to Will about his father's drinking, and Will unconsciously had decided to adopt Troy as his new little brother.

When Troy's father had awakened following a day in the ICU, it was Will who had stood next to Troy, hand on his shoulder, as Troy had struggled to restrain his tears of relief. And it was Troy who had showed up the following week at Carolyn's funeral, carrying a bouquet of pink roses and baby's breath, something Will was sure Troy really couldn't afford.

The next two years were difficult for Will and his father. The loss of wife and mother had left the two like a rudderless ship, drifting this way and that, influenced by whatever tides rose and fell, shifted and pushed. The loss of Patrick, such a pure and happy kid, had eaten away at them on a visceral level. Will was full of guilt, often despising himself in the dark hours when sleep wouldn't come. Bill worried constantly about his son but had little mental energy to devote to him. It took him almost every hour of every day just to keep his business afloat. Their lives seemed to be on a collision course that neither of them could stop, almost as if they were watching a train wreck in slow motion.

Chapter Four

Whaaanhh whanh whaaaanh! That familiar whistle sounded louder and more ominous. The rhythmic clatter of steel wheels over the track might have been peaceful in another scenario. Here, they grew louder and louder and louder until *WHAAANHH! CRASH!* and Will woke up screaming in his bed, his sheets soaked, images of his dead brother and mother tormenting him.

Will's grades had tanked after their deaths, although he had finished out the basketball season. Basketball practice and basketball games were the only times he could forget what had happened.

Counseling had helped some. After Carolyn's death, Will's father had been unable to pay their medical insurance bills and they had lost coverage, but Will was able to get help from school-based counseling through his school district.

Through weekly sessions with his counselor, a licensed clinical social worker named Judy Forrest,

Will gained insight, learned strategies for dealing with grief and depression, and discovered he had ADHD. Will had let go a huge metaphoric sigh of relief, finally understanding that his life-long disorganization and distractibility were not laziness or lack of caring, but a neurological-wiring issue. Judy had discussed with Will and his father an Individualized Educational Plan, an IEP for short, that could help Will stay focused and organized, finish his work, and turn it in on time. After balking initially, the school district's Child Study Team agreed to give Will an IEP, and his grades bounced back. He even gained academic ground. He began to heal, mentally and emotionally.

Will had many friends in school, particularly fellow athletes. He had always been gifted at sports, and this had still earned him praise and respect when he hadn't been measuring up academically. Will's relationship with Troy transcended even those long-term friendships. The two had bonded heart-to-heart in the hospital, although, being boys, they would have been hard-pressed to admit it.

As their relationship developed, Will instinctively understood that something in Troy was damaged in some way. That's why Will, easy-going, happy-go-lucky Will, a senior, deferred to Troy. Will enjoyed making Troy happy, being his big brother. It made Will feel good to fill a need in Troy's life. What he was unaware of was how much it filled the empty spots in his own soul. So when Troy had texted Will that

October Sunday evening, "Come pick me up," Will had grabbed his car keys and ran out the door. Ten minutes later, he had pulled up in front of Troy's house.

No sooner had Will pulled up than Troy slipped out of the house, letting the screen door slam shut behind him. He moved swiftly down the front sidewalk, hands tucked in the pockets of his zippered gray hoodie, his long, thick, curly hair catching the wind.

Opening the passenger door, Troy slid into the bucket seat. "Hey," he offered, stretching out his left fist to bump Will's fist. Although Will kept his grin to a friendly "hello," he couldn't help that his heart skipped a beat when his gaze met Troy's. There was sometimes something off about Troy's gaze, which Will caught again in the intimate glow of the overhead light before the younger boy shut the door.

Troy's voice startled him out of his momentary lapse in attention.

"I'm starved. Let's go up to Vinnie's and grab a few slices."

An observer might have smiled to see the two teenagers engaging in such typical activities: driving to the pizzeria, bantering back and forth, talking about girls, and eating pizza in a booth. Yet, while Will's red-and-white letter jacket, jeans, and ready smile projected an accurate first impression, Troy's slight stature and unassuming youthful appearance belied his churning conflicts inside.

Troy's real motive surfaced when he told Will they had a stop to make.

"Hey," he said. "We gotta drop by Ryan Sullivan's house on the way outta here. He owes me some money."

"Sure." Will slid out of the booth and picked up his cup of soda.

The two boys left the pizza shop and hopped into Will's car, parked right out front. Obtaining such a prized parking spot would never happen during the summer in Ocean Beach. After Labor Day, however, it settled back into its small-town feel.

There was a chill in the air that Sunday evening, and the first frost was expected by morning. Will and Troy cruised through the streets, listening to music on Will's Sirius radio. When they arrived at Ryan's, 15-year-old Ryan and his 17-year-old brother, Kevin, were standing on the front porch. Troy rolled down his window and called to Ryan, who ran down to the car.

"Hey, Troy. Hey, Will," he greeted them apprehensively as he leaned down into the passenger window. Although Ryan Sullivan knew Will Van Dalen on sight—who didn't? Will was a senior at Ocean Beach High School and a letterman on the varsity basketball team—he knew Troy much better. Ryan had developed a pot-smoking habit, and Troy was his dealer. Troy had readily supplied Ryan with enough bags of weed to create a sustainable habit, even allowing Ryan—and others—to forego payment at the time of delivery. Troy had discovered his customers would use more that way, and there was usually no problem collecting the cash later. Ryan was a little unnerved because, while Troy had been friendly and easy-going in the beginning, Ryan had fallen behind in his payments, and Troy had confronted him in the high school locker room.

The encounter had taken place the previous Monday toward the end of fourth-period gym as Ryan was changing from his gym shorts and T-shirt back into his street clothing. Ryan had sneaked out of phys ed class a few minutes early so he could meet his girlfriend before fifth period. Although the gym teacher hadn't noticed, Troy had.

As Ryan had put his left foot on the wooden bench that ran down the middle of the locker bank to tie his sneaker, Troy had suddenly appeared, edged up close to Ryan, and sat down with his legs on either side of the bench. He brought his face close to Ryan's. Troy didn't look high, but he didn't look normal, either. He was smiling, but the smile didn't reach his hazel eyes, which glittered coldly with an odd excitement. Troy was so close that Ryan could smell his breath.

Ryan was so startled at the swift, silent approach that he paled and straightened involuntarily.

"Hey, Troy," he faltered, offering a brief half-smile that did little to offset the cold fear that had balled up in the pit of his stomach.

"You owe me something, dude," said Troy quietly. "You gotta pay up." Ryan couldn't pull his gaze from Troy's glittering eyes.

"Yeah, Troy, I know. I'm sorry. I promise I'll get it to you by the end of the week."

Troy grinned even wider. "I'm sure you will, Ry. I'm sure you will. 'Cuz you know what will happen if you don't, right?"

Ryan didn't really know, but he nodded anyway, inadvertently backing away from Troy. "Yeah, yeah, sure, Troy."

Troy rose up off the bench, tossing a coin in his right hand. "See ya around, Ry."

As soon as Troy was out of sight, Ryan slumped back against the lockers. He was covered with sweat and his legs felt weak. He owed Troy a lot of money, and he wasn't sure where he was going to get it.

The jumble of this memory and the attendant fears and thoughts lay like icy slush in Ryan's stomach. *Two days late*, was all he could think. *Two days late, and I'm about to find out what happens when you don't pay up.*

Will, who'd pulled up to the curb in front of Ryan's house, watched the exchange without much interest. He was unaware of the amount of money Ryan owed Troy, or why, although were he to closely examine his own conscience, he'd know. He had heard stories about Troy, and his teammates had ragged on him about hanging out with the younger boy.

"Dude, what do you want with that kid? He's only a sophomore, but worse, he's trouble."

Will had downplayed their concerns. "Nah, it's like having a little brother. Besides, he's a good kid. He just needs a little looking after."

"'Good kid,' my ass. You'd better watch your back, Will."

Will hadn't really taken any of that seriously. *How bad could Troy be? Sure, he was a little rough, but that was from not having a mother around,* thought Will. Will himself had had an open and easy relationship with his own mother and had thought nothing of walking hand in hand down the street with her. No one ever teased him about it because it was so like Will, so sweet and open-natured, that even his peers got a kick out of it.

So when Troy told Ryan to "Hop in the back," Will had no concerns.

Troy turned to Will. "Let's take a ride over to the park."

Will shrugged, put the car in drive, checked the driver's side mirror, and pulled away from the curb. But after cruising no more than half a block, he was shocked when Troy suddenly leaped into the back seat. Keeping his eyes glued to the road, he heard Troy demand, "Where's my money? You said you'd have it by Friday. Now it's Sunday."

Terrified, Ryan replied between panting breaths, "I'm sorry! Troy, I'm sorry! I promise I'll give you the money! I swear it!" And then, "Don't! Please don't kill me!"

Will tore his eyes away from the road and looked into the rearview mirror. What he saw nearly made him crash into a parked car. Troy sat in the middle of the back seat, leaning in on Ryan with a knife to Ryan's throat. Ryan could only press back against the seat, eyes wide in pure mortal terror.

"Holy shit!" exclaimed Will. "What the hell are you doing, Troy?"

"Stay out of this, Will," answered Troy without turning his head or breaking his gaze from Ryan's face. "This is between me and Ryan."

"The hell it is, Troy! Get away from him!"

When Troy continued menacing the terrified

teenager, acting as though he were completely deaf to Will's protests, Will pulled over, leaped out, ran around the car, and flung open the back door. Without a thought for his own safety, he reached in and shoved Troy away from Ryan with the heel of his outstretched right hand, using his whole arm as a battering ram. He then grabbed Ryan's arm and hauled him onto the street.

Hitting the chill evening air, Ryan took off in the direction of his house. Breathing heavily, Will watched him run into the deepening twilight, the smack of his sneakers on the road's surface quickly receding.

Troy's voice in his ear startled him. "What the fuck did you do that for?"

Will spun to face him. "Are you kidding me? One slipup and you could've cut that kid's throat!"

"Shit, Will," said Troy calmly, staring at Will. "I never knew you were such a pussy. I wasn't gonna hurt him. I just wanted to scare him. I probably scared the shit right out of him." Troy grinned malevolently while he straightened the sleeves of his hoodie. "You're lucky I like you."

Will stared into Troy's face as Troy stared back, their breath mingling in the chill air.

Will broke the spell. "Let's get out of here," he said, moving toward the car.

"Thanks, Will. I think I'll just walk home. I'm only a few blocks away."

And with that, Troy walked silently through the glow of the corner streetlight and disappeared into the darkness on the other side.

Feeling suddenly cold and empty, Will climbed into the front seat of his Optima and shut the door.

Chapter Five

O*h god oh god oh god oh god* went the soundtrack in Ryan's mind as he raced the block back to his house. He could still feel the sharp blade of Troy's knife against his neck. The hair on his scalp was still raised. Although he was hardly aware of his flight path, his feet instinctively headed toward home and safety.

The porch light illuminated the front sidewalk, which bisected the neat lawn. Ryan barely registered any of it as he traversed the length of the sidewalk in one second flat, flying through the doorway and up the stairs to his second-story bedroom, letting the door slam shut behind him.

His brother was watching the Giants game on the TV in the front room off the hallway. Startled by the slammed door, Kevin yelled, "Jesus, Ryan!" as Ryan's feet pounded up the carpeted stairs. "What the hell got into you?" he said out loud in the empty room.

Kevin was in charge while his parents, Joe and Bette Sullivan, were out for the evening. The Sullivans liked to go out on a weekly date if they could manage it, grabbing dinner at Spike's Seafood then meeting friends at Joey's in downtown Ocean Beach for drinks, storytelling, and laughter.

When the boys were younger, Joe and Bette would hire a babysitter or, just as likely, Joe would bathe, powder, and pajama the boys while Bette cooked a special dinner that the two would share after the boys were tucked away for the night. The communication and pleasure helped to keep their love alive, encouraging their bond to grow deeper over the years.

Now that the boys were older, the Sullivans felt comfortable leaving them alone while they enjoyed a night out. After all, Kevin was a junior in high school, held down a part-time job, got good grades in school, and planned on becoming an engineer. Even if 15-year-old Ryan was a little less mature, they figured the boys were safe enough together, and they were only a phone call away should anything go wrong. They had no idea, as they laughed at the bar, eating peanuts and drinking the local microbrew, just how wrong things were going.

When Ryan didn't show his face after a while and the game was interrupted by a commercial, Kevin went upstairs to see what he was up to. He was surprised to find Ryan in his room with the door closed. Rapping twice with his knuckles, Kevin turned the knob and opened the door. Finding the room in complete darkness, Kevin was baffled. "Ryan?" he called out, reaching for the light switch. "Are you in bed?"

Light flooded the room from the overhead fixture, and Kevin saw Ryan huddled on the floor by the window, on his knees, head poking between the curtains, peeking out into the night. When the light came on, he jumped back and looked toward the doorway, white-faced. "Shut that off!" he yelled in a hoarse, strained whisper.

Kevin just stood there for a moment, staring at his brother, bewildered. "Shut that off," insisted Ryan, now backing away from the window. Kevin reached over and flicked off the light.

"Ryan, what's going on around here?"

"Nothing. It's nothing," said Ryan, taking fast, shallow breaths as he sat down on the floor with his back to the wall, his face barely illuminated by the glow of his computer screen.

"Oh, so nothing made you bolt into the house and hide up here in your room like it's a darkened cave? What happened, and why do you look like you just saw a ghost?"

Ryan sat still and said nothing.

"It was those guys in the Optima, wasn't it?"

"What guys?"

"Whaddayamean, what guys? That was Will Van Dalen's car. And that was that kid, Troy, with him. You know I don't like that kid. So, what happened?"

"Nothing happened, Kevin. I told you."

Moving swiftly, Kevin sat on Ryan's bed and leaned down into Ryan's face. "Ryan, you get into a car with a senior and Troy, the drug dealer—don't think I don't know it—and you come running back five minutes later looking scared shitless. Then you run upstairs, close yourself in your room, kill the lights, and you're peering out the window, looking— for what? So either I have my head up my ass, or something's going on. Since I don't have my head up my ass, you can tell me now, or you can tell Mom and Dad when they come home."

Ryan's head fell back against the wall, and he closed his eyes, exposing his youthful Adam's apple, which slowly dropped down and bobbed back up as he swallowed his anxiety, his frustration, his terror. He needed help. He knew that next time Troy wouldn't just scare him. He didn't have the money to give to Troy; he couldn't find a job at his age, and he hadn't been able to save his allowance to keep up with his weed-smoking habit. He suddenly felt very young again.

Dropping his head to bring his eyes level with Kevin's gaze, he took a deep breath. He couldn't see Kevin's expression in the muted blue light of his PC, but he sensed Kevin's patient expectancy coupled with a line-drawn-in-the-sand demand. He knew that if he didn't spill his guts now Kevin would force him to tell his parents later. And he was too frightened and ashamed for that.

"I owe Troy money," he muttered into the darkness.

"Money for what?"

How can I say it? he thought. He recalled the motto of the Nike ad he'd seen online: "Just do it." *Yeah*, he thought, *just do it*. He'd done it, all right.

"For *what*?" Kevin snapped.

"I bought some weed from him."

"Goddamn it, Ry!" Kevin exploded. "What do you need that for? You're an athlete. You keep smoking weed, you'll end up a nothing."

Kevin paused, emotion clearing and realization dawning.

"So… you owe Troy money, he comes by to get it, and now you're hiding in the dark. He threatened you, didn't he? What did he do?" Kevin demanded, then, more to himself, muttered, "That little pissant. Just wait till I get a hold of his puny little ass."

Ryan's eyes snapped open wide. "No! You can't! He'll just get angrier!"

"I don't give a shit if he gets angry," said Kevin.

"What's he gonna do to me?"

"He's got a knife."

"A knife?" Kevin hopped up and flicked the light on.

Both boys blinked as they adjusted to the new brightness.

"Maybe you'd better tell me exactly what happened." Kevin sat back down on the bed.

"Okay," sighed Ryan. He swallowed again, took a deep breath, and began. "When Will pulled up, Troy told me to hop in the back. He told Will to drive over to the park. Next thing I know, he's hopping in the back seat with me and holding a knife to my throat, screaming at me to give him the money I owe him."

"What was Will doing all this time?"

"At first, he was just driving. Then he started yelling at Troy to stop. Next thing I know, he stops the car and pulls me out onto the street. I started running and never turned around to look back."

"How much money do you owe him, Ry?"

When Ryan named the sum, Kevin whistled. "Holy shit, Ry. First thing you do is stop smoking weed. Next thing is decide what to do about Troy. The way I see it, we have three options. One, we pay him the money. Two, I beat the shit out of him and he goes away. Three, we report him to the cops, and he goes to juvie."

Ryan listened silently, wide-eyed, and marveled at his brother's intelligence.

"I have some money saved, so we could pay him off and end the whole thing. But I don't like that idea. I didn't work so hard to give it to a shit like Troy Braithwaite. Plus, if we do that, he'll keep selling drugs, and other kids will wind up in trouble. So... I could beat the shit out of him. While I would enjoy that, it could backfire on us. I'm a 17-year-old, six-feet, 180-pound football player. If I pound that little twerp into the ground, he could file charges against me, and the police could lock me up. So that's not a solution. That leaves telling the cops." Kevin looked at Ryan. "This involves Mom and Dad. You have to realize that."

"Geez, Kev, I really don't want Mom and Dad to know about this. They'll be so angry."

"They'll be a lot worse if Troy slits your throat, little brother."

Chapter Six

Driving home through the twilit streets, Will was on autopilot, barely aware of the turns and intersections he navigated as the whole scene played over and over in his mind: Troy suddenly leaping into the back seat. Ryan's terrified cries. The knife in Troy's hand glinting at Ryan's throat. Ryan's eyes bulging in fear.

As Will pulled into his driveway and killed the ignition, he sat for a moment, the dome light exposing his pale, drawn face to whatever was sheltered by the darkness outside. As the reality of what had just occurred crystallized in Will's mind, anxiety began churning in his stomach.

What will happen now? he wondered. Would Ryan tell his parents? How angry would Troy be and what would he do? Will felt the leaden weight of dread settle over him as he slowly removed his keys from the ignition, opened the door, and started up the walkway to the side entry. He hoped that, as the ocean breeze chased away the morning fog on the inlet, the whole thing would just blow over.

Chapter Seven

A couple of hours later, Ryan and Kevin sat with their parents at the kitchen table. The four had shared many a meal in the eat-in kitchen with its cheerful country rooster-and-hen wallpaper. The globe ceiling light glowed warmly, cocooning the clustered family but contrasting with the serious mood. Kevin had taken the initiative and called for a family meeting.

Bette, reading the unspoken gravity and concern that shadowed the faces of her sons, had put the kettle on.

Once they were all settled and clutching steaming cups of tea, it was Kevin again who acted as the spokesperson, bringing the parents up-to-date on Ryan's predicament. When he finished, Joe and Bette exchanged knowing looks, a mixture of fatigue, irritation, worry, and anger.

Joe put their thoughts into words. "Ryan, you know your mother and I love you. You also know you've broken our rules by using drugs. Naturally, we're upset about it, and we're going to deal with it. But first things first. This boy who threatened your life—that has to be dealt with immediately. I think we need to talk to the police about it."

Ryan looked up from his untouched mug of tea. "But Dad, if we go to the police, they'll find out I was smoking pot."

"They probably will, Ryan. But if we don't go to the police, this kid will continue to try to get money from you, and will try to harm you if you don't give it to him. Not only that, he'll continue to sell drugs to other kids and maybe threaten or hurt one of them."

Ryan stared down into his cup. "I guess you're right."

"So whaddaya say we head over to the police station before it gets any later?"

Ryan's head snapped back up. "You mean right now? *Tonight*?"

"Putting it off won't help set things right. Besides, there may be some evidence the police can gather now, when the trail is fresh."

Joe glanced over at Bette. "Why don't you and Kevin stay here, get ready for bed. We shouldn't be too long."

"All right, Joe." Bette smiled at him, and Joe

reached over and covered her hand with his own.

Joe glanced at the boys. "Ryan, grab your jacket and we'll head over."

"Okay, Dad." Ryan pushed back from the table, brought his cup to the sink, and walked out of the kitchen.

Joe stood, too, and put his hand on Kevin's shoulder. "I'm proud of you for doing the right thing. We'll take care of it. Now why don't you run up and take a shower so you can get some shut-eye?" He ruffled his son's thick, dark hair with a hand that was as large as it was gentle.

Bette smiled to herself as she rose, picked up the three remaining mugs, and carried them to the sink. She filled the sink with hot, soapy water and deftly rinsed out the mugs.

"Good night, Mom." Kevin kissed her on the cheek.

She returned the kiss. "Good night, Kevin. Have a good night's rest."

Joe came up behind her and put his hands on her waist. "What do we always say, Bette?" Sliding his arms around her, he encircled her while bending his knees behind hers and hugging her close. Then he answered his own question: "Parenting isn't for cowards."

"Good thing we're not cowards." Bette wiped her hands on the dish towel and turned into his embrace. "Do you want me to come with you?"

"No," he answered, briefly rubbing noses with her before stepping away. "You stay here and hold down the fort."

Chapter Eight

A few short moments later—too short, in Ryan's opinion—Joe and Ryan pulled into the parking lot of the Ocean Beach Police Department. Several black-and-white cruisers were parked in the lot at the rear of the low-slung, red-brick building. Ryan felt a sense of unreality, as if he were moving underwater. He could feel his heart pounding in his chest and his blood turning to ice in his veins. He had an urge to run, an urge he suppressed by reminding himself that he was headed toward safety. Or so he hoped.

Next to him, Joe switched off the ignition in the Oldsmobile Cutlass. "Come on, Ry," he said. "Let's get this over with."

Joe reached to open the driver's door, but Ryan made no movement, and Joe paused to turn to him. When their eyes met, Joe nodded once. By tacit agreement, father and son stepped out of the car. Shoulder to shoulder, they walked up the sidewalk. Stepping through the PD's front door, Joseph and Ryan Sullivan found themselves in a cubicle of a waiting room. A uniformed officer sat behind a window of bulletproof glass. The officer spoke to them through a speaker.

"Can I help you?"

Joe stepped up to the window. "Good evening, Officer. My son has some information about several crimes that were committed this evening. Is there a detective on duty we can speak to?"

The officer eyed them for a moment before picking up the phone and punching a few buttons. "Yeah, we've got an informant in the lobby. You wanna question him now?" The officer paused, then added, "Roger," and hung up the phone. "Officer Boyd will be right with you."

A moment later, the door to the left of the window opened, and a uniformed officer stepped into the lobby. He used an electronic wand along with a pat-down to ensure that Joe and Ryan carried no contraband or weapons. After he cleared them, he ushered them through the doorway. The click of the heavy door behind them resounded through Ryan's mind as he followed the broad back, uniformed in blue-gray, deeper and deeper into the PD.

They stopped at a gray cubicle, where they were met by another large man dressed trimly in a white polo shirt and dress pants. He was young, but his smooth face and brown eyes reflected a serious demeanor. Ryan was struck by the size and definition of the guy's bare biceps, which suggested he spent hours in the gym every day. The man reached past Ryan to grasp Joe's hand in his beefy one.

"How are you, sir? My name's Detective Graham, Kurt Graham."

"Detective. I'm Joe Sullivan. This is my son, Ryan."

Detective Graham gestured at two armless chairs alongside his cubicle. "Have a seat and make yourselves comfortable."

As Joe and Ryan pulled up the chairs, Detective Graham sat down in his own chair. He leaned toward them expectantly. "So, what brings you here tonight, Mr. Sullivan?"

Joe glanced at Ryan, who had remained silent and was now white-faced.

"Detective, Ryan told me a story tonight that disturbed me a great deal, and not just because of his role in the whole thing." He looked over at his son. "Ryan, I'd like you to tell Detective Graham what happened to you earlier this evening."

Ryan heard his father, but he was unable to speak. He couldn't see all that well, either. It was as if everything went dark all of a sudden, like the momentary blindness when you stand up too fast and you have low blood pressure. He heard a crackling sound in his ears. His mouth went dry and he couldn't utter a sound.

Then, the warmth and strength of his father's hand over his brought him back. He blinked and his vision cleared.

Joe turned to look at Graham. "Detective, could we have a glass of water?"

In the moment when the detective stepped away to the water cooler, Joe leaned toward Ryan and patted his hand twice. "Just take your time, Ry. It'll be okay. I'll be here with you."

Ryan swallowed. "Okay, Dad."

After he had sipped gratefully from the cold water, Ryan began to speak, haltingly at first, and then, gradually, the words and sentences formed themselves, tumbling and spilling out of him in a torrent. At first Detective Graham simply listened, but once Ryan relayed that Troy had held a knife to his throat, he stopped Ryan and looked at Joe.

"Mr. Sullivan, if you don't mind, I'd like to take a more formal statement at this time."

After Joe consented, Detective Graham led Joe and Ryan to their seats in an interrogation room. Detective Graham placed a digital recorder on the table and advised them that he would be recording the proceeding.

Detective Graham began: "Ryan, I'm Detective Kurt Graham of the Ocean Beach Police Department, and I would like to ask you some questions regarding a possible kidnapping, attempted robbery, and assault that took place at approximately six-thirty this evening on Niblick Street. Are you willing to make a voluntary and truthful statement about this matter?"

Ryan nodded.

Detective Graham advised, "You have to answer out loud so I can record your responses."

Ryan straightened in his chair. "Sorry."

Detective Graham took Ryan step-by-step through what had happened earlier that evening. Then they got to the cause of the dispute.

"Why did Troy want money from you?"

Ryan shifted his eyes back to Detective Graham. "I bought some weed from him. I had kind of gotten into the habit of doing it. The last time I wanted some weed from him, I didn't have enough money, but he said he would spot me the weed as long as I paid him by that Friday. But then I just didn't have the money."

"Okay, back to the car and the knife at your throat. What was Will doing while Troy held the knife to your throat?"

"He yelled at Troy, but Troy kept the knife at my throat and told Will to stay out of it."

"Then what?"

"The car pulled over all of a sudden, and I jumped out and ran down the street."

"Were you still on Niblick Street at that time?"

"Yeah."

"What happened next?"

"I started running and never looked back. When I got home, I ran right inside my house and hid in my bedroom."

"During the entire time you were in the car, did Troy stab you with the knife?"

"No, he didn't stab me, but he did push it up against my neck."

"Was that while he was threatening to kill you?"

"Yes, and screaming at me to give him the money."

"Did Troy make any other threats against you?"

"Just that he would kill me if I didn't give him the money."

"At any time during this incident, did Will Van Dalen make any threats against you?"

"Not directly."

"Were the windows open in the car?"

"No."

"Were the car doors locked?"

"Yes, I heard them lock as we pulled away from my house."

"Okay, Ryan. Is there anything further that you would like to add to this statement that you feel is pertinent or important?"

"No."

"Have you given this statement of your own free will?"

"Yes."

"Has anyone here coerced you or threatened you into making this statement?"

"No."

"To the best of your knowledge, have the answers been true and correct?"

"Yes."

"Okay, Ryan, we'll conclude for now." Detective Graham reached over and shut the digital recorder off. "After your statement has been transcribed, we'll call you back in to read it over and sign it."

The three stood up in the small room.

"Detective," said Joe. "What happens now?"

"We'll investigate the matter."

"As I'm sure you can imagine, I'm concerned about Ryan's safety. He goes to the same school as these two boys."

"We'll keep in touch, Mr. Sullivan. For now, Ryan should simply go about his business and keep away from Troy and Will."

Joe glanced at Ryan. "After this, Detective, I'm sure he will."

Chapter Nine

A fter Ryan and his father left, Detective Graham grabbed his jacket and car keys. He didn't need to look up Troy Braithwaite's address. He knew it by heart, since the kid had been on his radar screen for the last year. Per protocol, he advised his sergeant of his destination, then headed to Troy's home. Instead of simply calling Troy and asking him to come down to the station for questioning, he wanted to surprise the potential perpetrator.

When he rolled up to the house in his unmarked Crown Victoria, Graham saw a flick of the curtains in a front window. Probably a bedroom, he surmised, and was prepared for his knock to go unanswered. To his surprise, Troy opened the door himself.

"Troy Braithwaite? I'm Detective Graham of the Ocean Beach Police Department." He flashed his badge.

Troy glanced at it and waited, staring quietly.

"Are your parents home?"

"Nah. My father isn't home and my mom doesn't live here anymore."

"Would you mind coming down to the police department with me? You're not under arrest, but I'd like to ask you some questions."

Troy shuffled his feet a bit without meeting the detective's eye. Finally, he asked, "What about?"

"It concerns an incident with Ryan Sullivan and Will Van Dalen."

Troy stopped his shuffle and kept his head down a moment. Then he said, "Yeah, I guess." He shut the front door.

At the station, Graham whisked Troy through the corridors and into an interrogation room. He wasted no time setting up a recording device on the table between them. He went through the preliminaries, then began the interrogation.

"Mr. Braithwaite, I need to inform you of your rights." Detective Graham buzzed through the Miranda warning in a monotone voice.

Troy fidgeted in his chair.

"Do I need a lawyer?" he asked.

"That's up to you, son. I just wanna ask you some questions about a report I got earlier this evening about Ryan Sullivan and Will Van Dalen. I thought you might be able to help me. You know, kind of fill in the blanks for me and tell me your side of the story. Would you like to do that?"

"Um, I guess so."

"Okay, then I just need you to sign here, indicating that you understand your rights and you'd like to go ahead."

After Troy signed and Detective Graham took Troy's demographic information, Graham said, "I heard Will was driving the car."

At this, Troy's heart began to thud in his chest. *Holy shit, he knows what happened already.* Troy licked his lips. *But how much does he know?*

Detective Graham paused. One of the many tricks he regularly used was that most people can't abide silence and will usually try and fill it if you wait long enough. Detective Graham didn't have to wait very long.

"Yeah. Will was driving the car."

Despite Troy's outward attempt to play it cool, his face had gone pale and his breathing was shallow and rapid, two tell-tale signs that Detective Graham quietly noted.

Troy continued. "He came to pick me up and we got a slice of pizza. Over at Vinnie's."

"Then what happened?"

"Uh, Will swung by Ryan's house on the way home."

"For what reason?

Troy shrugged, his bony shoulders lifting his grungy black hoodie a couple of inches.

"I'm not sure, but I heard them talking about money. Will seemed pissed."

"Will was angry? About what?"

Troy pulled his gaze away and stared off into the corner, shaking his head slowly from side-to-side. "I'm not sure, but I think there mighta been some weed involved or something." Troy bit the cuticle on the side of his thumb, eyes skewing off to his left.

"Yeah, Will told Ryan to hop in the back, and then he just took off down the street. Ryan was like, 'Dude, where're we goin'? I gotta be home when my parents get there.' Then Will was like, 'Dude, you can go home when you give me what you owe me.' And Will pulled over to the side of the road. I just hopped out on the corner and walked home from there."

"You just got out and left?"

Troy nodded his head. "Yeah, man. Things were getting too weird."

"Did you see anything further? Or hear anything?"

"No, man, nothin'. I just went home."

Chapter Ten

After charging Troy with assault with a deadly weapon, Detective Graham left Troy in a cell waiting for his father to pick him up. Since he was a juvenile, he would be released to his father's custody. Graham didn't care all that much about prosecuting Troy. Graham knew that the narcotics team had been keeping Troy under surveillance since the summertime, hoping to nab the drug suppliers who were higher up the food chain. With Troy loose, they'd continue to watch him. Graham had his own burning reason for focusing on Will Van Dalen, however. Will was a thorn in his side, an irritating canker sore that just wouldn't heal. In high school, Graham had tried out for varsity basketball, but he never made first string and spent all the games on the bench. It didn't matter how many hours he spent in the gym or on the court shooting baskets. He just didn't have Will's natural talent, or good looks. Although he wouldn't admit this to himself, he was jealous of Will's easy success on the basketball court and on Will's good looks and popularity. Consequently, he lost no time driving the short distance to Will's house. When he pulled up in front of the two-story, gray Victorian, he saw a silver Optima in the driveway, a good indication that Will was home. Since a few lights were still lit despite the late hour—it was almost midnight—it appeared that at least someone was awake.

When Detective Graham rang the doorbell, Will opened the door.

"Hi, I'm Detective Kurt Graham of the Ocean Beach Police Department." He flashed his badge. "I'm here to speak with Mr. Will Van Dalen. Are you Mr. Van Dalen?"

The young man's eyes widened as he stared at Detective Graham. Standing in his stockinged feet on a wooden floor, he was speechless. After a moment, he found his voice. "I'm Will Van Dalen," he said.

"Mr. Van Dalen, I have information that you were involved in an incident this evening on Niblick Street that also involved Troy Braithwaite and Ryan Sullivan. Is that true?"

Despite Will's relative naiveté, he knew enough to ask, "What incident?"

The detective's impassive expression didn't waver. "Mr. Van Dalen, were you with Troy Braithwaite this evening?"

"Yes, at least for part of it," Will answered.

"I'd like you to come down to the police department

to answer some questions. You can ride with me in my car."

Will hesitated. *Dad's asleep. Maybe I can get this over with without his knowing.*

Detective Graham stood perfectly still, gazing at Will. The sheer size, presence, and authority of the police officer convinced Will to do as he asked. Leaving the inside door open, Will grabbed his jacket off the coatrack in the hall, stuffed his feet into his signature red, size-11 Converse sneakers, then pulled the door closed behind him.

Detective Graham strode wordlessly to the car with Will keeping pace. As they approached the black, late-model Crown Victoria, the detective unlocked the car door with his key fob, gave Will a pat-down, and bent down to open the back door. Hands in the pockets of his high school letter jacket, Will climbed inside and Detective Graham closed the door behind him. As Will sat in the back of the detective's car, alone in the late-night darkness, a frisson of fear shot through him. Ice filled his veins.

After a silent ride to the station, Detective Graham led Will inside. Will followed Graham to an examination room deep inside the building and sat at the table indicated.

Detective Graham spoke as he placed a digital recorder on the table and activated the power button.

"Mr. Van Dalen, at this time I'd like to take a formal statement from you."

"About what?" asked Will.

By way of answer, Detective Graham proceeded through the opening protocol and the Miranda warning.

"Now, knowing these rights," he said, "are you willing to answer my questions freely and voluntarily and without the presence of a lawyer?"

Will responded, "Am I being charged with a crime?"

Detective Graham replied, "Right now, Mr. Van Dalen, we are investigating the possibility that crimes were committed in town this evening. You are simply a person of interest at this time. I'd like you to assist us with this investigation. That's why I asked you to come down here. We already have some information relating to the incident that occurred. I'd like to get your side of the story. Are you willing, at this time, to answer my questions freely and voluntarily?"

"I just don't know if I need to have a lawyer."

"Mr. Van Dalen, you are 18 years old, correct?

"Yeah, I turned 18 this school year, and I'm a senior in high school. I play varsity basketball, and I'm hoping to get a scholarship to help pay for college next year. My dad can't afford to send me without that. His business has been in trouble since my mom died, and everyone goes to Home Depot and Lowe's now. He's really struggling to pay the bills. If I get in trouble, I don't know what will happen. I don't want to get into trouble."

"Well, that's up to you. I'm asking you to cooperate with me so I can investigate what happened. You can help me do my job by telling me everything you know about the incident. I already have a statement from two witnesses, so this is your opportunity to tell your side of the story of your own free will. You are here to assist the police. If you become uncomfortable at any time, you can stop me. That's your right. But it would certainly help me and benefit you to tell your side of the story. Would you like to do that?"

"Uh, okay."

"Then I need you to sign right here. This says you were advised of your rights."

After all the preliminary information was recited for the record, Detective Graham said, "Okay, Mr. Van Dalen. You know I'm interested in what happened tonight when you were with Troy Braithwaite and Ryan Sullivan. First, tell me how the three of you happened to get together."

"Troy called me up and asked me to go for pizza. I picked him up and we went to Vinnie's for a couple of slices. While we were there, Troy told me he had to stop by Ryan's house, so I drove him over there."

"You were driving the car, correct?"

"Yeah."

"And the car belongs to you?"

"Yeah, it's my car."

"Did you go straight to Ryan's house?"

"From Vinnie's, yeah."

"And where is Ryan's house?"

"On Niblick Street."

"What time was that?"

"I don't know, around six-thirty, I think."

"Okay, and was Ryan at home when you got there?"

"Yeah."

"Are you friends with Ryan?"

"No, he's a freshman."

"Is Troy friends with Ryan?"

"Not really. I don't think so."

"Mr. Van Dalen, I'm confused. If you're not friends with Ryan, and Troy isn't friends with Ryan, why did you go to Ryan's house?"

"Troy had something he wanted to talk to Ryan

about."

"Are you sure? Wasn't there something you had to get from Ryan?"

Will's brow furrowed. "No, sir. Ryan didn't have anything of mine. Troy asked me to swing by Ryan's house."

"Okay. Did you and Troy go up to the house when you got there?"

"No, Ryan was on the porch, so Troy called him over."

"Okay. So, Ryan came over to the car?"

"Yeah. Then Troy told him to get in."

"And did Ryan get in your car at that time?"

"Yeah."

"So where was Ryan seated when he got in your car?"

"He climbed into the back behind Troy."

"What happened next?"

"Troy told me to drive over to the park."

"And did you?"

"I started to, but we never got there."

"Why not?"

During the interrogation, Will had been hunched over in his chair, forearms leaning on his knees. The interrogation had fallen into an easy rhythm. At this point, however, he hesitated and glanced up at Detective Graham.

"Mr. Van Dalen, remember that I already have the statement of a witness. It really is in your best interest to tell me everything you know."

Will looked back down, letting his gaze fall to the floor. "Well, as I was driving down the street, Troy jumped into the back seat and started yelling at Ryan, and Ryan started screaming and yelling."

"What was Troy yelling?"

Will hesitated for a moment.

Detective Graham was silent, waiting.

"Troy was saying Ryan owed him money."

"And what was Ryan screaming about?"

"He was yelling, 'Please don't kill me!'"

"What did you say to Troy about killing Ryan?"

Will looked up, startled. "I told him not to kill Ryan."

"You just wanted him to scare Ryan?"

Agitated, Will jumped to his feet and started to pace. "No! I had nothing to do with it!"

On high alert, Detective Graham straightened up to his full seated height. "You were driving the car, correct?"

Will started running his hand through his hair. "Yeah, I was driving."

"Ok, what happened next?"

"I looked in the rear-view mirror and saw Troy holding a knife to Ryan's throat."

"You saw Troy holding a knife to Ryan's throat?"

"Yeah."

"What kind of a knife?"

"I'm not sure."

"Okay, how big was the knife?"

"I'm not sure."

"How did you know it was a knife? What did you see in the mirror?"

Will hesitated again. "I saw the metal blade against Ryan's throat. I guess it was about three inches long."

"Okay. What happened next?"

"I yelled at Troy to get away from Ryan."

"Did he listen to you?"

"No," said Will. He was staring into the corner, eyes unseeing, focused inward. "I kept yelling at him, but he didn't stop."

"Then what happened?"

"I pulled over, got out of the car, opened Ryan's door, shoved Troy off of Ryan and pulled Ryan out of the car."

"What did Troy do then?"

"Ryan went running down the road. Troy just kind of laughed it off and went home."

"And what did you do? Did you drive Troy home?"

"No, he walked home."

Detective Graham leaned toward Will, his figure intimidating yet somehow also comforting in its nearness. After all, he was a police officer, charged with upholding the law. Will knew he would get to the bottom of what happened, and everything would get straightened out.

"C'mon, Will. You know as well as I do what this is all about. Ryan owes money for weed he bought. It's not a joke." The detective's voice took on a sarcastic tone as he continued, "You guys swing by Ryan's house on the way home from Vinnie's pizza. Ryan isn't your friend, he's just a ninth-grader, and he isn't Troy's friend. He was buying weed. The question is, who was he buying it from? You or Troy? Your friend Troy is a drug dealer. We know that. We've been watching him already."

Will's head snapped up to meet Graham's gaze.

The detective looked back intently into Will's eyes. "That's right, Will. But you're older than he is, and you two hang out together. A senior and a sophomore. Kind of unusual, wouldn't you say?"

A pause fell over the room, then Detective Graham said, "Troy's in trouble, and you might be in trouble, too, if you're not careful. He's going down over this. Don't let him take you with him."

"But Troy's just a kid..." Will's voice faltered.

"He's a 16-year-old male who was present at an incident involving the sale of illegal drugs to a minor, then said minor was kidnapped at knifepoint. That's a succession of serious crimes. You're already involved because the incident this evening happened in your car."

Will's stomach clenched into a ball. Even though he'd been dreading something bad happening after the evening's events, he hadn't imagined things would go this far. After all, he hadn't done anything wrong. Had he?

"Mr. Van Dalen, in concluding your statement, were you threatened or mistreated here this evening by anyone present?"

"No."

"Has your statement been given of your own free will?"

"Yes."

"Have the answers you've given been true and correct to the best of your knowledge?"

"Yes, sir."

"After this statement has been transcribed and you have the opportunity to read it or have it read to you, and you find it to be true and correct, will you sign it?"

"Yes." Will paused. "Will anyone else get to read this? Like, is Troy allowed to read my statement?"

"Once your statement is typed up and you sign it, it will go to the prosecutor's office. If charges are filed against Troy Braithwaite, there is a chance that he or his attorney, if he has one, will read your statement as part of discovery in the case."

"Oh, man."

Detective Graham reached over and turned off his digital recorder.

"At this time, Will, I'm going to excuse myself for a few moments. Do you need to go to the men's room before I leave?"

"Oh, no, thanks. I'm okay."

"Can I get you a drink of water?"

"No, thank you."

"Okay, then, just sit tight and I'll be back shortly."

Detective Graham exited the investigation room, shutting the door behind him. He stopped by his sergeant's desk with an update.

"Hey, Sarge, I just finished questioning one of the perps in tonight's kidnapping incident. I have enough to write up an arrest affidavit and submit it to the judge for a warrant."

"Okay, Graham. Where's the perp?"

"He's in the investigation room. I think he'll be okay there."

"Does he know he's being charged?"

"Not yet."

"All right. Just give us a warning before you spring the news in case you need reinforcements."

With that, Kurt Graham headed to his desk to draft the arrest affidavit. He included facts gleaned from his questioning of Ryan, Troy, and Will. Will Van Dalen would not be happy. Detective Graham had enough evidence to seek charges for assault, aggravated assault, conspiracy, attempted robbery, and kidnapping. Even though some of the details were still murky, the statements all established that Will was an adult, he had driven his car to Ryan's to extract money in return for a controlled dangerous substance, had locked his car, in which Ryan had been detained and assaulted, and he had confined Ryan, a minor, to his personal vehicle against his will.

Once Graham was finished, he faxed his affidavit and request for the arrest warrant to the judge on duty. It was returned within ten minutes. After alerting the sergeant, Detective Graham went to break the news to Will.

Chapter Eleven

Will had been sitting in the uncomfortable chair now for almost an hour. Restless and anxious, he had bent the single paper clip he had found on the table in one direction and another until it snapped in his fingers. It lay there, irreparably broken.

Just then, the door opened and in walked Detective Graham. A uniformed officer walked in behind the detective. Detective Graham took the only other seat, while the officer remained standing. They'd left the door open.

Sensing a shift in approach, Will looked apprehensively from detective to officer and back again. "What's going on?" Will blurted out. "What's happening?" He knew he was breathing heavily, but he couldn't seem to get his breath. He began to panic. He hopped up out of the chair so he could pace off his excess energy, but there was no place to go. The officer uncrossed his arms and backed up, blocking the doorway.

Will turned wide eyes on Detective Graham. "Am I under arrest?"

Detective Graham remained seated. "Mr. Van Dalen, please calm down. Everything's fine. Please have a seat."

"Everything's fine? It doesn't seem fine to me. What's going on? You brought me down here so I could make a voluntary statement. You didn't tell me I was under arrest!"

"And you weren't under arrest," said the detective calmly. "But I did read you your Miranda rights because, as I explained to you at the time, you were a person of interest in several crimes that were committed in town this evening."

"And I answered all your questions. I told you the truth!" Will's voice rose in desperation. He sensed, rather than understood, what was happening.

"Mr. Van Dalen, I need to tell you that you are being charged with the following crimes: assault, aggravated assault, conspiracy, attempted robbery, and kidnapping."

Will's mouth hung open.

"I have a warrant for your arrest. You will be fingerprinted and held in a cell here until transfer can be effected to the county jail."

"I have to call my dad!"

"You will be allowed one phone call at some point."

"But I can't go to jail! I'm a high school student! I'm on the basketball team. I can't go to jail."

"Officer O'Leary will take you in and get you fingerprinted."

The uniformed officer stepped forward and took Will by his left bicep. "Please come with me, Mr. Van Dalen."

Will turned and looked at the officer as his feet, as if controlled by another force, began stepping forward, one after the other. He walked with the officer to the fingerprinting area, where Will was printed, photographed, and booked for the crimes. As the officer was settling Will behind the bars of an internal jail cell, Will, who had remained mute throughout the process, regained his voice.

"Officer, I have to call my dad."

Officer O'Leary paused. "Alright, Van Dalen. Come with me."

The officer led Will to a nearby desk. "Have a seat."

Will sat down.

Officer O'Leary picked up the phone, punched a few buttons, and got a dial tone. He handed the phone to Will. "Here you go. This is your one phone call, so make it good."

Will grabbed at the phone as if it were a life preserver. He pulled the chair up closer to the desk, dialed his father's number, and—wrapped in the gauzy surrealism of the moment—alternated between feeling relief and terror.

He could hear the phone ringing at the other end. Ringing and ringing. *Where was his father?* Of course, it was nearly one-thirty in the morning; his father was probably sound asleep. Will could only hope he would answer.

Just when his hope was virtually extinguished, Will heard the ringtone break off and an abrupt "Hello."

"Dad…?" Will breathed, more in disbelief than in supplication.

"Hello?" said his father, now more questioning than angry.

"Dad, it's Will."

"Will? What's going on? Are you okay? Where are you?"

"Dad, I'm at the police station. I need help."

"Police station! What on earth are you doing at the police station?"

"I've been arrested."

"Arrested! Have you been drinking?"

"No, Dad. Can you come down here?"

There was no immediate answer. Will held his breath.

"I'm on my way."

Will heard the *click* of his father hanging up.

Will lifted his eyes to Officer O'Leary, who was looking on silently. Officer O'Leary's eyebrows and mouth frowned in unison. "Okay, son,

let's go." The officer escorted Will back to the cell and locked him in.

Will sat down to wait.

Chapter Twelve

Bill Van Dalen drove through the darkened October streets like an automaton. He had seen enough life in his forty-eight years not to be surprised by much, but at the moment, he was shocked. Never had he expected to be summoned to the police station to pick up his son Will. Will had always been a happy-go-lucky kind of kid, never mean, never in trouble. Oh, sure, he had his issues. What teenager didn't? But Will had always been a good, friendly, well-behaved kid. He was a little goofy and unfocused at times, but he was so good-natured that no one ever held that against him. He did well enough in school and, if he wasn't a rocket scientist, he was a hard worker, a B-C student. He would have done better if he could maintain his focus, but that seemed like a lost cause at this point. He was easily distracted, and he could never find anything in his book bag or in his room. But he had passed his core-curriculum subjects and, boy, could he play ball!

After Will's mother, Carolyn, and his brother, Patrick, had died in the train wreck two years earlier,

Will and his father had been left suddenly alone together. It was hard for Bill to manage the home, his business, and Will on top of it. Not to mention how completely adrift he felt himself. As if the world had simply imploded, leaving a gaping silence. A few months after Caro and Pat had died, Bill's sister, Dana, had pulled him aside one weekend and given him a piece of her mind.

"Can't you see that boy's depressed?" she asked. "He needs to see a counselor."

"What are you talking about, Dana?" Bill asked. "He's going to school. He does what he has to do. He's fine."

"Sure he is, just like you're fine. Admit it. Neither one of you is eating right. The house is coming apart. Your business is suffering. You've lost at least twenty pounds. And Will is withdrawing from his usual activities."

Bill started to protest out of habit, but his conscience smote him. Maybe, in his own grief, he was overlooking the needs of his son. He heeded his sister's advice and looked into the school-based counseling offered at the high school. There, he found a clinical social worker, Judy Forrest, to provide counseling. Judy was someone with whom Will could connect and share his burdens. He'd had to bite the bullet there; the revenue from his business had fallen off since Carolyn and Patrick's deaths and he'd had to cut costs somewhere. Unfortunately, the somewheres had added up, and he'd let go of all their medical insurance. There was no room in the budget for the luxury of psychotherapy. Luckily, their school district had school-based services, which included counseling.

Counseling had provided more benefit than Bill could have imagined. After a couple of weeks, Judy Forrest had asked to meet with him.

"I'm concerned about Will," she had volunteered without preamble on the night of their meeting. "He's definitely depressed, a condition I believe is a result of the deaths of his mother and brother. He's lost weight, has some trouble sleeping, and feelings of helplessness and fear. However, I think he also has an attention-deficit disorder. Through my initial clinical interview and rating scales, I've found that he demonstrates many of the common signs and symptoms."

Judy continued, "I asked Will to bring in his homework. His backpack was a mess! His assignments were poorly organized, and he often makes careless mistakes. He gets lower grades than he deserves."

Bill searched Judy's face as she spoke. "What can we do about it?"

"I'm suggesting that we ask for evaluation by the Child Study Team to see whether Will is eligible for special education and related services," said Judy.

"But Will's not a special ed kid." Bill was more baffled than angry. "He's not retarded or slow."

"Exactly right," said Judy. "Which is why he should be doing better in school. Students who have a disability, like ADHD, that adversely affects their academic achievement are allowed to have a special program in school. It's called an IEP. The school can then make modifications for Will that will help him to be more organized, less distracted, and to learn better."

"But won't he feel singled out, like special ed kids? He won't like that."

"I've already talked with him about the types of assistance he could get in school, and he seemed interested, even excited, about it."

"What exactly could they do for him in school?"

"He could get all kinds of organizational tools and training, and he might even need some one-on-one assistance with a special education teacher. That's a teacher who could help him to organize not only his homework, but also his approach to classwork, projects, and scholarly papers. I think it could make a world of difference for him." Judy paused. "What do you say?"

"It sounds great, but how do we get this plan for him? Do I have to do anything?"

"Someone has to refer him to the Child Study Team. You can do it, or, if you'd like, I can do it for you. In fact, the Child Study Team is more likely to agree to the evaluation sequence if I carefully present, in writing, the reasons we're asking for it."

"If that's the case, then please go ahead and do that as soon as you can."

Now, even as he steered his car in the direction of the police station, Bill wondered: *Could the ADHD—and the depression—be the reason Will ended up in police custody?* He also wondered, as have most parents from time immemorial, *Have I been missing something? Have I not been paying attention?*

The irony of that "attention" question brought Bill back to reality. *But I* did *follow through*, he thought. *We* did *get him classified as Other Health Impaired, and we got an IEP. Should we have done more? Should I have trusted the Child Study Team as much as I did?*

Despite the gravity of these ponderings, Bill ran out of time to consider them further—he'd arrived at the police station. The chill, early-morning air seeped into his bones as he rushed from his car into the building. He walked directly up to the intercom in the lobby, just as Joe Sullivan had only hours before.

"My son's been arrested," he said to the officer

manning the front desk.

The officer met his gaze, betraying no emotion. "Name?"

"My son is William Van Dalen, Jr. Will for short. My name is Bill Van Dalen."

"How can I help you?" asked the officer.

"I'd like to see him," said Bill, frustrated.

The officer made a phone call. After he hung up, he said, "We have no visiting hours here, sir. Your son will be brought to the county jail as soon as transport can be arranged. You can go to the indictment and the bail hearing in the morning."

"Bail hearing! What are we talking about here? And why wasn't I called?"

"Apparently you *were* called, sir, otherwise you wouldn't be here. Your son is an adult, so we have no obligation to notify anyone. Prisoners are allowed a phone call, and your son was given that courtesy."

"My son is a high school senior! He's a kid! Of course, I should be called."

The officer behind the glass simply stared at Bill.

Bill passed his hand over his face and paced in a small circle once around the lobby.

"Look, Officer, is there any way I can see my

son, just talk to him briefly?"

"It's not protocol, sir."

Again, Bill's hand wiped the frustration from his countenance. He worked hard at keeping his cool.

"Officer, do you have children?"

Again, he faced the silent sentinel.

"Officer, I'm reduced to begging you. That boy you have in there may be 18 years old, but emotionally, he's no adult. Please, please, would you make an exception?"

The officer sighed and picked up the phone again. "Yeah, I need somebody up front here. Yeah, thanks." He hung up. "Somebody'll be right with you."

Bill hung his head and squeezed the corners of his eyes, his nose burning. He managed a subdued "Thank you."

A moment later, an officer entered the lobby and searched Bill, then led him back to see Will. The shock of actually seeing his son locked up in a jail cell was more than Bill was prepared for. Rooted to the spot, he stood stock-still.

Far from paralyzed, Will sprang to the bars and wrapped his fingers around them. "Dad!"

"Will, what happened?"

"Oh, Dad, it's so stupid! I didn't do anything wrong! I swear!"

Will's eyes slid over to the uniformed officer standing just behind his father.

Bill turned around. "Is there anywhere we can talk alone?"

The officer led them to a plexiglass cubicle where attorneys questioned their clients. The guard could see them but not hear their conversation. Will had to be shackled to the tabletop by one arm. Bill sat across from him at a fast-food restaurant type of table.

Bill just looked at Will for a moment. "Okay," he said. "Let's take this from the top. How did you end up here?"

Will proceeded to give his father a brief summation of the night's events.

"Damn it, Will, I thought you were smarter than to hang out with kids like that. You know what they say—you lie down with dogs, you get up with fleas."

"But Dad, I had no idea that Troy had a knife."

"Let's not think about that right now. We have to figure out what to do about this." Bill was silent for a moment, intent on his thoughts. Then, he looked up at Will.

"You're supposed to be brought to the county jail

for a bail hearing later this morning. I'll call Mr. Fennelly. He'll know what to do. Maybe he can meet us in court and represent you."

"Okay, Dad. Thanks."

Chapter Thirteen

By the time Bill Van Dalen arrived home, it was nearing three-thirty in the morning. Since the last thing he felt like doing was sleeping, he put together a plan to free Will from jail and exonerate him of the charges. Neither he nor anyone in his family had ever been on the wrong side of the law, and he was confident that, presented from the right angle and with the appropriate legal representation— that is, Will's godfather, Declan Fennelly—this could all be put behind them. Will would learn a lesson about whom you could really trust in this world, what kind of friends could lift you up, and what kind of "friends" could bring you down.

Bill made a list of things to do. First, he would have one of his managers open up the lumber store and landscaping shop and keep the jobs moving this morning. The next thing to do was to find out how to handle the bail hearing. Declan was the only attorney he knew. He'd helped Bill incorporate his business and had drawn up his and Carolyn's estate paperwork. He trusted Declan so completely that when Will was born Bill had asked Declan to be the godfather.

Since those tasks were isolated and the plan was in place, Bill put on a pot of coffee and sat down at the desk in his home office to get ahead on his company paperwork. He had a hard time concentrating, however, since it seemed that life was battering him from all sides. His business had never done as well as he had planned, and with the big-box stores opening more and more locations, his store was slowly sinking. After Carolyn's and Patrick's deaths, he had worked on in determined fashion for Will's sake, but the fire had gone out. He was merely forcing himself through the motions.

At 6:00 a.m., Bill called the lumber manager and alerted him that Bill had a pressing family matter to attend to and that he'd need to come in early to keep things on task.

Since it was still too early to call Declan, Bill sat down in front of the TV. His heart nearly stood still when, there on News 12 New Jersey, his favorite blond reporter was covering an 18-year-old Ocean Beach man who was being held, pending bail, in the county jail after allegedly kidnapping and assaulting a local teenager. Worse yet, Will's name—and high school photo—were plastered all over the screen for the entire viewing public to see.

"Goddamn it!" yelled Bill into the empty house.

He jumped up angrily, still staring at the screen, unsure of his own intentions. Before he could make up his mind, the phone rang, jarring his already-frayed nerves. He snatched it off its charger in the kitchen. Seeing his sister's number on the digital readout, he rolled his eyes heavenward.

"Can this day get any worse?" he asked an unseen, unnamed deity.

"Good morning, Dana," he said evenly into the phone. He willed calm into his bones as his sister demanded to know what happened.

"I just saw Will's name on the news. What on *earth* is going on, Bill? It can't be true!"

"Well, yes and no, Dana…" he began.

"Yes and no! What kind of answer is that?"

"Just calm down and listen." Bill sighed and collected his thoughts. He experienced a brief and oddly misplaced urge to laugh at his and his sister's tendency to be such early risers, a habit inherited from their Dutch forebears. "I didn't finish. Yes, the answer is yes and no. Yes, Will did get arrested, and he was charged with kidnapping." Bill heard Dana's sharp intake of breath. "No, because Will didn't do anything wrong. Anything, that is, except get mixed up with the wrong friend."

"What does that mean?"

"It's kind of a long story, Dana, and I've had a rough night. I've got a lot of things to take care of today, as you might imagine."

Dana's voice softened. "Of course, you do. It's just that I've been so worried about Will since Caro and Patrick died—and now *this*." She paused and her silence spoke volumes. "Bill, if there's anything we can do, just let me know. Do you have a lawyer?"

"I'm just waiting for a respectable time to call Declan Fennelly."

"Don't wait! Call him! What's he there for if he can't help you at a time like this? I'm sure he wouldn't mind if you called him on his cell phone."

"All right, Dana, I'll call right away." Bill rubbed the back of his neck with his free hand.

"You keep me posted, y'hear?"

"All right, Dana, yup, I will." His sleepless night catching up to him, Bill was eager to get off the phone. After he hung up, he glanced at the digital clock over the stove. Six-twenty-two glowed on its face. He had to call Declan. If he waited any longer, they might not make the bail hearing.

Bill pulled his cell phone out of his pocket and pressed the number for Declan's mobile.

Declan answered on the second ring, sounding as if it were midday and a phone ringing at this hour was normal. Bill quickly brought Declan up to speed and asked whether he could represent Will at the bail hearing that morning.

"Sure, Bill," he said. "I have to be at the courthouse this morning anyway. It won't be any trouble. I'll swing by and have the law clerk put a ready-hold on the matter, and I'll come by just as soon as I'm done putting in an appearance before Judge MacAllister."

Something loosened inside of Bill's guts and he felt a rushing sense of relief. He hadn't realized how much he was depending on Declan to get Will out of jail.

After they hung up, Bill grabbed his navy sport coat and a conservative tie to wear with tan dress slacks. He pressed each garment on the ironing board in the kitchen. It was moments like this that had his heart aching for Carolyn and Patrick. It was hard to parent alone, to face the world without a wife, to cope with the grief and "what ifs" inflicted by the death of a child. It wasn't that he couldn't do things for himself—he and his siblings were raised to be independent—it was simply the complete absence of a partner, a helpmeet (a good, old-fashioned word), especially when she was the woman he'd loved for decades, a helpmeet who'd been his best friend and had loved Will as much as he did.

But Carolyn was gone. Patrick was gone. And nothing would bring them back. He would do as the

British did and just get on with it.

After a quick shower and a shave, Bill grabbed another cup of coffee and a toasted bagel. By the time he finished, it was time to leave for the courthouse. He hopped into his Chevy Tahoe and pointed it south.

Twenty-five minutes later, Bill was nosing into the parking garage opposite the county justice complex. The complex housed not only numerous courtrooms, but the county jail and sheriff's offices as well.

After clearing security and finding out that Judge Giordano was holding the bail hearings, Bill got directions and proceeded down the winding staircase into the main hall of the complex. Upon locating Judge Giordano's courtroom, he found the door locked, so he took a chair against a wall. The hallway was majestic with a cathedral ceiling, but dingy as well, stained with the remnants of passion, greed, anxiety, and sorrow. Even now a human tide ebbed and flowed up and down the echoing corridor.

The cumulative anxiety in the hall increased Bill's own nervous energy. The relief he had felt after speaking with Declan only two hours earlier was gone. He suddenly felt very much alone. His wife was dead. His only remaining son was locked up somewhere inside this very courthouse, and all Bill could do was wait for help. He felt out of his element and powerless. The legal system seemed an unfathomable, impenetrable morass. He'd rather be doing *anything* other than sitting here, waiting for a bail hearing—except Will was in there somewhere, alone, confused, and scared. He straightened himself in his chair.

As if good things really do come to those who wait, Declan Fennelly appeared at that moment. Bill stood and the two men shook hands. Considering the respective sizes of the men, an observer might have thought Bill the more capable. At six feet, two inches tall and a shade over 200 pounds, Bill was no lightweight. Declan was shorter and wirier, with curling auburn hair shot with gray. Declan's slight stature and affable appearance belied an incisive and quick mind, however. If he didn't bring the luck of the Irish, he brought to his clients the loquacious vivacity of his forebears. His quiet smile extended to his twinkling eyes as he looked over his long-time client and friend.

"Good morning, Bill."

"How are you, Declan?"

"Right as rain, I am, Bill. Don't you worry. We'll take care of that son of yours. I got here early so I could see Will before the proceeding. I had to hear the story from his own mouth."

Bill was barely able to register his surprise. "How

was he? What did he say?"

Declan relayed Will's answers, then Bill took a few moments to give Declan the rest of the facts regarding Will's situation, Declan nodding all the while. Shortly thereafter, the bailiff unlocked the courtroom door, an action that triggered the movement of the human herd that had gathered. Declan led Bill to a seat on the front bench, then stepped through the bar and chatted up the court clerk. Bill had to work to keep space open on the bench since people were squeezing into every space imaginable. After all the seats had been taken, they lined up against the walls.

When Declan returned and sat next to Bill, he leaned over and said, "They'll be bringing Will in soon, Bill. I want you to be prepared. He'll be wearing an orange jumpsuit and he'll have his hands shackled."

Bill's eyes widened. "Is that really necessary? Isn't that prejudicial or something?"

"The state has the right to ensure the safety of the public, and Will is charged with some serious crimes. It's just part of the process, Bill. Try to think past it."

A few moments later, the door to the right of the judge's bench opened and a uniformed sheriff's officer came through. Following him was a line of men in orange jumpsuits. They shuffled in, single file, and filled the jury benches. When Will stepped through the door, his eyes connected with Bill's. Bill felt it all the way down in the pit of his stomach.

After the men were seated, the court clerk stepped through the doorway and called, "All rise. His Honorable Hugo Giordano presiding."

The judge swept into the room in his black robes. As he took the bench on the dais, he called out, "Please be seated."

The judge turned to the PC on the bench to his right and logged on. The court stenographer had taken her seat and had already started recording the proceeding. The room's yearning eyes were fixed on the judge, in whose hands their lives were held at this moment in time.

Declan hadn't wanted to tell Bill that Judge Giordano had a nickname: Judge Hugo-to-Hell, since he often handed down the longest sentences permitted by law.

Judge Giordano looked up and addressed the court room. "Court is now in session." His glance turned to the assistant prosecutor at the plaintiff's table.

"Good morning, Ms. Foster. I have today's roster here. My clerk has indicated which cases have defense counsel present, so I'll start with those."

Bill sat, tense, listening for Will's name. The judge called first one case, then another, dispensing with each either through a release on bail or remanding the prisoner to jail. Suddenly, it was Will's turn.

"State v. Van Dalen."

Declan rose from his seat, made his way to the defendant's table, and stood before it.

"May I have your appearances for the record," said the judge.

"Lori M. Foster for the State of New Jersey," said the assistant prosecutor.

"Declan Fennelly for the defendant, William Van Dalen, Jr."

The judge nodded at Declan, who sat down, then indicated with another nod at the assistant prosecutor that she could proceed: "Ms. Foster."

"Thank you, Your Honor. The defendant is charged with several very serious crimes: assault, aggravated assault, conspiracy, attempted robbery, and kidnapping. The aggravating factors include the victim's age—he is only 15. The matter involved the sale of a controlled substance. The defendant was driving the getaway car and locked the car doors so the victim could not escape, while his accomplice attacked the victim with a knife in the back seat of the car. Therefore, the state is asking for $500,000 bail." Foster sat down at the plaintiff's table.

Declan stood, adjusted his suit jacket, and

addressed Judge Giordano. "May it please the Court, Your Honor; Ms. Foster is overzealous in her request for bail. The defendant, Will Van Dalen, is only 18 years old. He is a high school senior, captain of the varsity basketball team, a good student, and he's never been in trouble before in his life. For all intents and purposes, even though we call him 'Mister' now that he has turned 18, he is still a boy. He was giving a friend a ride when, at the friend's request, they stopped at the alleged victim's house. Also at the friend's request, the alleged victim climbed into the back seat of Will's car of his own volition. When Will proceeded down the street toward the park— again at the friend's request, and without protest from the alleged victim—the car doors locked the moment he took his foot off the gas pedal. It's a safety feature of the car that he drives. He did not purposely imprison the other high school student in the back seat. With his close community and family ties, he is not a flight risk. Therefore, Mr. Van Dalen is respectfully requesting that Your Honor release him into his father's custody without the need for bail."

After what seemed to Bill an endless moment, the judge spoke. "Given the gravity of the charges, the court cannot release Mr. Van Dalen without bail. However, I will reduce bail to $50,000."

Declan stood again. "Thank you, Your Honor. On the defendant's behalf, I am requesting that the defendant be required to post only 10 percent."

"The request is granted, Mr. Fennelly, but if Mr. Van Dalen fails to appear in court when summoned, take note that the entire amount will become due and owed immediately."

"So noted, Your Honor, and thank you." Declan nodded at Will, then approached Bill. "You'll need to go upstairs and post bail."

Bill stood and followed Declan out of the courtroom.

Declan turned and said, "I'll show you where you post bail, then you can pick Will up at the back of the jail on the other side of the building."

Bill walked back up the stairs with Declan. They stopped at an upstairs office. "This is it, my friend. They'll tell you what to do here." He turned to go.

Bill was beginning to feel desperate again. Almost breathless, he strode after the lawyer. "Declan! Wait!" When he caught up to Declan, he asked, "What's going to happen now?"

Declan recognized the abject terror that often gripped his clients. He checked his own impatience. "The court will set a trial date about four weeks from now. We'll need to meet prior to that date to discuss the possibilities. Why don't you call my office after you pick Will up, and my secretary can schedule you to come in?" Declan smiled.

"All right. I'll do that. Thanks." The two men shook hands and parted. Bill turned back to the window to post Will's bail and find out where he could pick his son up. He then retrieved his car from the parking garage and drove to the jail exit. It didn't seem to be the right place; there was a large sloping driveway that led to industrial-size doors with a loading dock to one side. But that's where he had been instructed to wait. Bill parked on the street and turned off the truck's engine.

Sure enough, after about 10 minutes, the door on the loading dock opened and Will appeared in front of two sheriff's officers. They closed the door behind him. Will, in the same jeans he'd worn last night, looked around in bafflement. Catching sight of Bill's Tahoe, he broke into a run.

Upon reaching the door, he flung it open and jumped inside, exclaiming, "Dad! Dad! Thanks so much!" He flung his arms around Bill in childlike exuberance and relief. Then the memories of the last 12 hours rushed back and closed over him, changing his initial exuberance to shame, withdrawal, and embarrassment. He pulled back, hung his head and said, "I'm really sorry, Dad. I didn't think I did anything wrong. I didn't commit a crime; at least, I didn't mean to."

Bill reached over and patted him awkwardly.

"Let's get out of here and get a bite to eat. Then we'll talk about what to do next."

Father and son drove along Route 57, a six-lane highway cutting east-west through East River, which offered a large choice of fast-food restaurants. They ordered from a drive-through window and headed home.

As they downed their burgers and fries, Will spoke up.

"Is Mr. Fennelly going to handle my case?"

"We'll have to talk to him about exactly what's going to happen," answered Bill. "But, yes, he's going to take care of this for you. For us." Bill gave Will a smile of encouragement, which Will returned.

After a moment of silence, Will said, "Dad, I can pay for it. I'll pay my own legal fees."

In his throat, Bill felt a tightening born of both pride and sorrow: pride for Will's grown-up offer to take responsibility for what had happened, for what *was* happening, sorrow for the fact that it was happening at all and even—he hadn't really admitted this to himself, yet the questions lurked deep in his mind—for the possibility that he himself was to blame somehow, for missing the possible connection to Will's depression, and the possibility that his son's attention-deficit disorder may have interfered with his judgment. He was also fearful of the potential legal costs, but he'd worry about that later.

"Will," he said, "I appreciate your offer, but I'd rather you put your time into your studies and basketball. We've talked about it before, and you know how I feel about it. You're the best ballplayer they have in Ocean Beach, and having a good season may put you in a position to get a full ride to college. That's worth more money than whatever you might earn to pay Mr. Fennelly. I want you to stay focused on your future." Bill cleared his throat. "It's what your mother would have wanted, too."

Both father and son silently struggled with their emotions for a moment. Then, in a subdued voice, Will said, "Okay, Dad. That's what I'll do."

Chapter Fourteen

The faculty at Ocean Beach High was abuzz over the news reports. "Will Van Dalen!" they exclaimed in the staffroom.

"I don't believe it," said his Algebra Two teacher.

"No way! Not Will," said another.

"It can't be true," said other staff members.

"How could a kid like Will do such a thing?" the teachers asked each other.

The administration and central office staff were even worse, gathered in the old, wood-paneled conference room, pouring coffee, gathered 'round the hometown paper at the conference table. There, on the front page, was Will's picture above the fold: *Local Basketball Hero Arrested* in 20-point type, and, underneath in smaller type: *Community in Shock Over Kidnapping*.

Naively, neither Will nor his father were prepared

for how fast the news had spread. After their morning in court, they had decided that Will would shower, change, and go straight to school. That way he could attend the rest of his classes for the day and legitimately show up for basketball practice. Bill had even written an excuse for Will to hand in to the main office, citing an important appointment. Then Bill changed and headed to work to determine whether things had gone according to plan that morning. Before he left the house, though, he had made an appointment with Declan for Wednesday evening. He wanted to ensure he and Will were ready for whatever they had to face.

Feeling self-conscious, Will dropped off his note in the main office before heading to class. Although he was aware of some restraint on the part of the main office secretaries, he tried to tell himself that he was just imagining things. After all, it had been a strange night followed by a strange morning.

Will tried hard to keep his mind on his classwork, but that was impossible given his new notoriety. Some of his classmates sneaked glances at him, and he noticed more whispering than usual during classroom instruction. A couple of his teachers pulled him aside to ask what had happened. Although he was polite, he kept his answers simple. He felt awkward under this unwanted spotlight.

A couple of his closer classmates grabbed him at his locker before eighth period.

"Will, what the hell happened, dude?"

"You really got arrested? Did you spend the night in jail?"

"It's all that scumbag Troy's fault. I told you to stay away from him."

After a quick rundown of how he'd spent the last 24 hours, he split from the group to head to his last class.

At the end of the academic day, Will went to the locker room to change for basketball practice. The jousting and good-natured ribbing that regularly took place there fell silent upon Will's arrival.

"Hey, guys," Will said as he began twirling the dial on his combination lock.

Suddenly, the locker room erupted with noise and movement. Will's teammates crowded around him, jostling him and asking questions. One of Will's closest friends, senior Howie Mays, moved the closest. A tall redhead who played forward to Will's point guard position, Howie asked, "Will, bro, what's goin' on? There's some bullshit story going around that you're Troy Braithwaite's drug dealer and that you were so pissed at Ryan Sullivan for flaking out on Troy that you beat the shit out of Ryan at the park. Other people are saying Troy's got some kind of dirt on you and he's blackmailing you."

Will's head drooped and his shoulders slumped. Expelling a breath, he said, "That's just fuckin' ridiculous."

"I knew it. I knew it," cried Liam McDonough. "I knew that shit wasn't true."

"But, Will," Howie continued, "you were all over the news today. My mom even saw it on TV. What the hell happened?"

Will leaned back against the lockers as he huffed out a breath.

"Man, where do I start?"

He quickly gave them a run-down of the past 24 hours as his friends closed ranks in an unconscious show of support.

Each of Will's teammates had something negative to say about the rumors, and something positive to say about Will and how the truth would prevail. As they continued, the commotion reached a deafening roar.

"Will." Coach Lichtenberg's authoritative voice rang from the doorway, silencing the group.

Will met the coach's gaze.

"I'd like to see you in my office."

That doesn't sound good, Will thought. Eyes unfocused, Will shut the door of his locker and walked toward the coach's office.

Coach Lichtenberg sat behind his desk, gathering his thoughts. All he could think about was the discussion he had had earlier that day with the school principal, Joe Anderson. He had listened incredulously while Joe related the story about the kidnapping and assault, about Will's arrest, and about the consequences the school was meting out. Due to the gravity of the charges against Will, and because he was an adult, the school was suspending him for 15 days. Joe also mentioned that some members of the Board of Education were pushing for expulsion. Given Will's good standing as a student and on the basketball team, Joe had prevailed upon them to keep it to suspension for 15 days. As a result, Will would not be permitted to participate in any school events, including athletic games and competitions, during that time.

It couldn't have happened at a worse time, thought Coach Lichtenberg. Will was arguably the best player on the high school basketball team, and now the team would have to play without him. *That could ruin our chances of reaching the finals in our division*, he thought. *But, if Will is out of school any longer, or, God forbid, the Board of Ed manages to expel Will, it will ruin his chances of getting into college.*

The coach had gotten so caught up in these thoughts that he hadn't noticed Will standing in his doorway.

"Excuse me, Coach," Will began.

Coach Lichtenberg just stared at Will for a hard moment. *He's just a simple kind of kid,* thought Lichtenberg. *Guileless and good-natured. He's no drug dealer.* The coach's gaze swept over Will, a clean-cut, polite kid who looked pretty downcast at the moment. *Not an adult*, thought Lichtenberg. *And not a kidnapper. Not this boy.*

He sighed. "Will, come on in. Shut the door and have a seat." The coach fussed with the paperwork on his desk for a moment, then dropped his hands into his lap. He looked up at Will. "There's something I have to tell you."

Will waited expectantly.

"Principal Anderson came to see me this morning. The police notified him about your arrest and the charges filed against you."

Will shot to his feet. "What?" he exclaimed. "Why did they do that? What does that have to do with school?" Will stared, hands planted on the coach's desk, mouth and eyes wide.

"Unfortunately, Will, it has a lot to do with school."

"But how? Why?" Even in his anguish, Will's youthful demeanor shone through in his face.

"Sit down, Will, and I'll tell you about it."

When Will was seated again in the chair across from him, Lichtenberg told Will about the agreement between the local police and the school. "School districts and local police in New Jersey have formal agreements. The schools and the police share information about students who bring drugs to school, or weapons, or who get into trouble. It's supposed to keep the student body safe. It's usually a good idea."

Lichtenberg continued, "In your case, Will, it's having an unfortunate effect." The coach paused. "The principal advised me that you're being suspended for fifteen days."

Will gasped.

"You know what that means, Will. You can't play basketball for fifteen days."

Will's face turned white.

"I can't believe this," said Will softly, almost to himself.

Lichtenberg's heart lurched as he watched his young superstar felled like a young sapling in the forest. He tried to shuck off the dreadful feeling that had come over him.

"Will, take it easy. It's early in the year. The fifteen days will pass by and you'll be back before you know it." Coach decided not to add to Will's burden by telling him the board was pushing to expel him. *What good could that do at this point?*

"Will," he said a little more sternly so Will would snap out of his mood. "Listen to me. I want you to go home now. I want you to stick with your workout schedule. Go out for a run this afternoon. I don't want you losing your stamina and then coming back here in three weeks all fattened up from too much pizza and TV. And keep up with your schoolwork. Go to your locker, get all your books, and try to stick with the assignments your teachers post online."

"Okay, Coach." Will looked pale and dazed. He got up slowly.

"Will, I want you to call me every afternoon and touch base. You check in with me so you can stay up to speed. You hear me?"

"Sure, Coach." Will gave him the ghost of a smile. "Thanks."

Lichtenberg watched Will disappear in the direction of his locker. *I've got a bad feeling about this*, he thought.

Chapter Fifteen

Will this nightmare ever end? Will trudged to his locker to get his books. He felt as if he'd entered an alternate universe, like something out of a horror movie, like he could see a place yet could not touch it or return to it. He walked through the school building, barely noticing the few students who remained in the halls.

Dumping his book bag in the back seat of the Optima, Will climbed behind the wheel and started the engine. He felt a nameless, swirling anxiety as he drove home through the familiar streets. Suddenly, he was no longer Big Man on Campus. He wasn't captain of the Ocean Beach basketball team. He wasn't the golden boy he'd been just twenty-four hours ago. Instead, he was just a kid who had gotten suspended from school.

Like any derelict stoner who doesn't give a shit about school, his family, or his life, Will thought.

Will suddenly felt a rage rise up inside of him.

He felt like screaming and smashing the dashboard. Flooring the accelerator. He didn't give in to those urges, though, because overriding all of them was the numbing fear that he was no longer in control of his life. So, he tamped down his emotions, went home, and fell asleep on top of his bed without taking off his sneakers or jacket.

Chapter Sixteen

The phone rang at five-thirty, waking Will out of a dead sleep. It was his dad.

"Hey, Will, I'm gonna be stuck in the office for a while longer. I've got some pressing paperwork to finish."

He didn't want to tell Will just how pressing.

"Can you manage dinner for yourself?"

"Sure, Dad," he said, rubbing his hand roughly over his face to help him wake up. "No worries. I'll see you a little later."

"I won't be too late." Bill hoped that was true. In reality, he was sweating over the bills, trying to figure out a way to increase his customer base. Things were looking pretty bleak.

Chapter Seventeen

A fter the call with his dad, Will rolled over and went back to sleep.

Bill was surprised to arrive home and find no lights on. It was getting dark by five-thirty these days, and it was now close to eight p.m.

Will's usually home at this hour, Bill thought. *But then again, so am I.* He tried to keep some semblance of a routine going for Will's sake. He knew enough about raising kids and modern psychology to understand how important it was to have regular meals with your kids. It wasn't just the meals; it was the stability of the regular routine, the place you belonged in the world, and the communication that happened over a meal that all contributed to a kid's safety and welfare. It helped to keep them away from drugs and casual, unprotected sex. In Will's case it seemed to have worked—until yesterday.

Bill parked the Tahoe in the garage and entered the kitchen through the garage door, snapping on lights as he went. Will's car was in the driveway, but he was nowhere to be found. The house felt deserted. Will's book bag was at the bottom of the stairs, where he usually dropped it, but there was no jacket or sneakers by the door. However, neither was there a note saying where Will had gone.

Oh, well, Bill thought. *Will often didn't remember to write notes. Why should tonight be any different?*

But tonight was *different,* thought Bill. *Tonight was the night after Will had been arrested for a series of very serious crimes. The least he could've done was to let me know where he is.* Bill felt a stirring of resentment about literally being left in the dark at the end of such a day. He climbed the stairs to change his clothing and wash up before he hunted up some dinner.

At the top of the stairs, he glanced down the hall. In the faint light from the hallway, Bill could see Will lying on the bed in his room. Startled, he walked softly along the hallway, coming to a standstill in the doorway of Will's room. There was his 18-year-old son, sound asleep in his red-and-white letter jacket, body splayed out in surrender. Bill's heart tightened, and some deeply-held part of his being cried out against the unfairness of life.

Where was this boy's mother? he raged to himself. *Why did she have to die and leave them alone? Why was his son arrested when he had done nothing worse than be in the wrong place at the wrong time? Was it just this morning we were in court?* It felt as if it had been days ago. *And how could anyone treat this boy like an adult, this teenager who, in reality, was just a simple, good-natured kid?* Bill could see him at other times in his mind's eye, his big, friendly smile plastered all over his face. *He was never one to get into trouble,* thought Bill. *Only forgetfulness at times and a little mischief.*

Just then, Will moaned in his sleep. Bill considered letting him find escape in the land of dreams, but then he heard his own mantra: *Just get on with it.* It was better to face things head-on, face them down, and conquer them. Besides, if the moan was any indication of the type of dreams Will was having, they weren't much of an escape. Better to wake him and face things together.

Bill walked in, laid a hand on Will's shoulder, and shook him gently. "Will," he said softly. No response. Bill shook him a little harder, but Will didn't stir. "Hey, Big Guy, wake up. Let's you and me get some dinner."

Will finally lifted an eyelid.

As his eye focused, he recognized his dad's shape in the semi-darkness, and he awoke fully all at once.

He closed the eye again and went into a full-body stretch, complete with a yawn. Then his body went limp.

Memories of his interview with Coach Lichtenberg flooded his mind.

"I'm not very hungry, Dad," he said with his eyes shut.

"C'mon now, Will," Bill chided jovially. "You've gotta keep your strength up and stay on schedule."

"Maybe later, Dad."

"Seriously, son. I know it's been a rough 24 hours, but you can't let this thing get the better of you. You have to keep up your schoolwork and stay physically and mentally fit. You're working for your future here, son."

Cold to his bones, Will rolled onto his back and stared at the ceiling. "The future's not lookin' so good right now."

"What are you talking about?" Bill frowned. "You're gonna have a good season—it's your senior year. You're captain of the team. You'll earn a scholarship if you handle that ball the way you always have."

"I may not have that chance, Dad."

"Why not?"

"I got suspended today. Fifteen days. I can't play or even practice while I'm suspended."

"Suspended? For what?"

Will looked up at his father. "Coach Lichtenberg told me the police have to notify the school when a kid gets arrested. So Mr. Anderson and the board decided to suspend me for three weeks."

"Holy shit." Bill sat down abruptly on Will's bed. He felt blindsided. *I never even thought of school*, Bill thought. "Can they even do that?"

"Apparently," said Will.

Bill felt as if he'd hit a brick wall. He tried to come up with a way of attacking the problem, but the fatigue of a missed night's sleep, coupled with his own worries and stress, was taking its toll on him.

"Will, let's take this one thing at a time. What did we learn from Judy, hmm? H-A-L-T stands for *hungry, angry, lonely, tired*. All my lights are lit on that scoreboard, so let's go get something to eat. Whaddaya say?"

"I think I'll skip *hungry* and just go straight to *tired*." Will rolled back onto his stomach, shoving his pillow lengthwise under his body and head.

As his body stilled, Bill gazed down at him but didn't have the wherewithal to push any harder. He stooped over and untied Will's sneakers, pulled them off, and dropped them onto the carpet. Reaching over, he rubbed Will's soft buzz cut. "Good night, son. Sleep tight."

"Don't let the bed bugs bite," returned Will quietly, a sweet throwback to childhood.

Leaving Will to find what solace he could in sleep, Bill headed toward the kitchen. He peered into the freezer through falling clouds of chilled vapor and shuffled items around until he unearthed something suitable.

Several minutes later, Bill had a freshly nuked dinner in front of him on the kitchen table. The glow of the overhead light illuminated him as he consumed his solitary sustenance. On the table next to his plate lay a copy of *Popular Mechanics*. Usually a temptation for Bill, who tinkered a little in his spare time, the magazine lay unopened and unexamined, the swanky sportscar on the cover completely unappreciated. Instead, Bill ate his meal in silence.

He remembered visiting Carolyn in the hospital the day after Will had been born. Their baby had been born on a sunny Sunday afternoon in October, a day full of promise and happiness. *Sunday's child is full of grace*, thought Bill. And Will had been a delightful infant. Long and lean at birth, he grew into a chubby two-year-old who noticed everything around him. *How long ago and far away it all seems. And now here we are, alone together. I've tried to be a good father,* he thought. *But right now, it doesn't feel so good.*

Bill tried focusing on a solution to Will's situation. He reviewed the steps he'd already taken and thought ahead to their meeting with Declan. He felt a renewed hope from these simple acts, and he resolved to get a good night's rest and keep moving forward.

He swept his leftovers into the garbage with a fork, stowed his dirty dishes in the dishwasher, and wiped down the table. After showering briefly and checking on Will—sound asleep and breathing deeply—he set his alarm for 6:00 a.m. and got into bed.

Chapter Eighteen

When the *gronk! gronk!* of the alarm sounded the next morning, it was still pitch black, and Bill felt as if he had just closed his eyes. Normally a cheerful riser, Bill had the urge to pull the covers over his head and hide in his bed for just a bit longer.

Now there's a juvenile reaction, he chided himself. *Who's the adult in this house, anyway?*

Throwing back the covers, he rose and went about his morning routine, shaving, ironing his clothes, packing his lunch, and making his breakfast. Bill normally included Will in the work and morning meal. This morning, however, he decided he'd let Will sleep in. Leaving a note on the kitchen table reminding Will to eat his breakfast, do his chores, and whatever schoolwork he had, he let himself out of the house.

It wasn't until a few hours later that Will awoke, groggy with too much sleep. Reality settled in as soon as he was conscious, its leaden weight keeping his body pinned to the bed and slowing down his mind. Without realizing how quickly the minutes were slipping by, Will lay on his bed for another half an hour. Eventually, his stomach sent *empty* signals to his brain and he, seeing the hour, forced himself into the bathroom to drain his bladder and wash his hands.

Still clad in yesterday's clothing, Will went quietly into the deserted kitchen and found his father's note on the table. He poured himself a glass of orange juice and pulled a Pop-Tart out of the box. Eyeing it critically, he bit into it cold.

To hell with the egg whites and oats that Coach wants us to start the day with, he thought. *What difference does it make now, anyway?*

Although, deep down, he knew this was a defeatist attitude, he couldn't summon the energy to care. Still munching on the Pop-Tart, which might have been cardboard to his tongue, Will sat at the table and started playing video games on his cell phone. He had barely lifted his head for the next hour and a half when the telephone startled him.

Grabbing the phone from its charging stand, he saw the name of his dad's company on the readout. He punched the *talk* button. "Hey, Dad."

"Hey, Will. Just checking in to see how you're doing."

"I'm okay."

"Did you see my note?"

"Yup." Will scratched his head and paced the kitchen in a circle.

"Did you do the things I asked you to?"

"Some of them."

"Which ones?"

"I had breakfast." Will said, grinning in spite of everything.

"That's a start. Why don't you check your schoolwork on Star Portal and get that done? Maybe go out for a run afterward?" Bill was a firm believer in keeping busy.

"Okay, Dad."

"Oh, and when's your next appointment with Judy?"

"I… I don't know."

"Check the calendar. We usually write it down, and you usually go on Thursday afternoon." A pause. "Tomorrow, we're going to see Mr. Fennelly at five, so don't make any plans."

"Where would I go?"

"Will."

"Okay, Dad."

"See you tonight."

After hanging up, Will went to the PC in his bedroom and logged onto the school district's website. Through a program called Star Portal, he could access the classwork expected of him for the next week—that's if the teacher had posted the work, of course. Most of the teachers were pretty good about it.

Will found he had math problems to do, some reading for English, and the outline of his research paper in psychology (the paper itself was due next week). He blew through the equations, then pulled out his copy of *Hamlet* and flopped down on his bed. He slogged through about twenty pages before returning to his desk to get started on the outline for psych class.

He was sure he'd put the paperwork in his book bag, but he couldn't find it. He ended up dumping everything onto his bed and going through the books and papers one by one. Somehow, it had disappeared.

Oh, well, he thought. *I'll just go for a run instead.*

He couldn't run at the high school track since he wasn't allowed on school grounds. He put on shorts, a T-shirt, a lightweight jacket, and his sneakers, then headed out the front door and started running toward the boardwalk.

That's one of the great things about living near the beach, Will thought. *You could just go up there at any time, day or night, spring, summer, winter, fall.*

The Atlantic Ocean and the beachfront had their own personalities and their own beauty in every season. The water today was fresh and clean, with lively waves and whitecaps, spume whipped up by autumn gusts. The crowds had thinned since the summertime, but some of the stores and restaurants were open year-round, and there were plenty of people—and seagulls—out and about. Handymen were putting new coats of paint on the buildings to freshen them after a summer of searing sun and to protect them from the winter winds. Plumbers were clearing the pipes so they didn't freeze in the months to come. Older couples walked slowly along the boardwalk, enjoying the space and the sunlight.

Will took all of this in as he ran and felt better than he had since his life had more or less imploded less than 48 hours earlier. In the sunshine, his youthful legs pumping, arms swinging, he couldn't help but have his spirits lifted. For the first time, he felt hopeful.

Falling into his usual rhythm, he ran to the southern end of the boardwalk, turned around and headed north toward the inlet, then down around Channel Drive and through the neighborhoods. He ran for a full hour, and when he got home, he'd worked up an appetite.

After eating a turkey sandwich and showering, his mood still elevated, Will logged onto the school's website and checked to see whether his lost outline might have been posted online. Voila! *Bless Dr. Farley's heart*, thought Will. *There it is*. He printed out a copy and reviewed it.

Initially tickled with the ghoulishness of the characters, Will now felt uneasy as he confronted the task. He wasn't sure how to begin the paper. It had to be a minimum of four and a maximum of 10 pages.

A truck rumbled down the street, and Will got up to look out the window. He could see the driveway, the front yard, the front sidewalk, and the road in front of the house. The truck was nowhere to be seen.

Will returned to his chair. *Okay*, he thought. *I'll look at my notes.*

He grabbed his psychology notebook and thumbed through it. He had pages of notes on anxiety disorders, mood disorders, psychotic disorders, and personality disorders. His own anxiety made his stomach clench. His notes swam in front of his eyes. He tried to remember what Judy, his counselor, had taught him about dealing with anxiety: "don't just do something, sit there." It turned the original maxim on its ear. The trick was to stop and really *think* instead of rushing around and fueling the anxiety.

Will tried to practice what he'd learned, but the

elevated mood spawned by his long run in the fresh air and sunshine had evaporated. In its place was the churning anxiety he now felt. He tried to just sit and think, but confronting his difficulty beginning this project—a difficulty he'd always had—just made it worse. His mind then began spinning into more discouraging thoughts. He didn't feel right sitting in his room on a Tuesday afternoon when he should be at basketball practice. The guys were counting on him this year, and now he was letting them down. They kept texting him, asking when he was coming back and if his dad was getting anywhere with the lawyer.

What a punk they must think I am to get involved with Troy! Unconsciously, he crushed the psychology outline in his hand. He threw the paper ball into the garbage and began to pace his room. He grew more and more uneasy, feeling like a wild animal in a cage. His heartbeat and respiration had increased, although he wasn't aware of it.

He had to bust out of the house.

He ran downstairs and grabbed his car keys. Revving the Optima's engine felt good. The engine itself felt powerful, something Will envied. He backed out of the double driveway and headed off to nowhere in particular.

He soon found himself in front of Troy's house. He hadn't made a conscious decision to drive there, but now he was curious: What the hell had happened to Troy? He parked the Optima and headed up the sidewalk. Before he could knock on the door, it was flung open and there stood Troy.

"Oh, look who it is—my friend the narc," Troy said sarcastically.

Will stopped on the sidewalk in front of the low front porch, confusion wrinkling his brow. "What are you talking about?"

"Oh, now you're gonna be all cute with me and act like you know nothing." A vicious smile twisted Troy's lips. "You ratted me out, Van Dalen. You're a pussy. Just like you've always been."

Will didn't get into fights easily, but he was in no mood for insults, especially from a kid he'd treated like a younger brother. He took a step forward, raised his arm, and punctuated his sentences with a pointed finger at Troy.

"You have no business accusing me of being a narc. You know as well as I do that I've been a good friend to you, even when you didn't deserve it. Now my ass is in hot water because of *you*! And you have the balls to stand here and accuse me of being a narc!" Will dropped his arm. "Think again, buddy. If you're in trouble, it's your own fault and you know it. You should be apologizing to *me* and promising to tell the cops the truth—*I* didn't kidnap Ryan Sullivan.

The only reason I even went near that kid's house is because you asked me to. Whatever shit you got going on between you and Ryan is yours. Do you know I got arrested for what you did? I could end up in jail! This is serious, Troy."

During Will's tirade, Troy had leaned his lanky body against the doorframe and stuck his hands into the pockets of his jeans. He gave every appearance of being unconcerned with Will's problems. When Will finished talking, Troy said, "Holy shit, Will. I love the way you play innocent." He shoved himself upright off the doorjamb and stepped out onto the porch so he and Will were only a couple of feet apart. "You knew exactly why I wanted to go to Ryan's house that night. Don't pretend you didn't."

Will's eyes bugged out. "That's the worst bullshit I've ever heard, Troy, even from you. You know better than anyone I had absolutely nothing to do with your little deals and your sleazy business." He stepped a little closer, bringing his face inches from Troy's. "My friends warned me about you. They said you were trouble, that I should watch my back. And I stuck up for you, you little bastard." Will clenched his teeth. "I stuck up for you! But they were right. You're more trouble than you're worth."

Will couldn't have known that those words struck a deeply resonant and ugly chord inside of Troy. His mother used to say the same thing as she stood in front of a mirror, applying lipstick: "You're more trouble than you're worth, Troy." Then she'd go off to who-knew-where, until she had left for good. Those words had festered inside him and tapped into a well of hatred.

Will stared at Troy another moment; Troy stared back, his face carved of granite, hatred glittering in his eyes.

"Don't ever call me again," Will said. "And don't ever tell anyone you're a friend of mine. You aren't." With that, Will strode back down the sidewalk, hopped into the Optima, and peeled away from the curb.

Chapter Nineteen

Troy saw the Optima's brake lights brighten as Will got to the corner and heard the tires squeal as Will ripped away from the stop sign. A cool wind whipped around him, whooshing over his shoulders and inside his collar. Troy barely registered any of this, though. He still stood, immobilized by the reverberating voice in his head: *You're more trouble than you're worth, Troy. You're more trouble than you're worth, Troy. You're more trouble than you're worth, Troy.*

Rage welled up inside him, directed not at the woman who had damaged him as a child, not at the object of his unconscious fantasies of maternal love, but at the friend who had abandoned him.

Will should have stuck by me. He shouldn't have told the cops what happened. I shouldn't have been questioned by the cops. I didn't do anything wrong. Ryan owes me money, and he has to pay. Will fucked this all up by letting the kid get away.

Not for an instant did he admit that he himself was responsible for setting the whole incident with Ryan in motion. He let his deep hurt fuel his anger.

Propelled by the intensity of his anger, Troy slammed into the house and started tearing through his closet. He had a handgun hidden there, a Lorcin P25 .25 caliber pistol, wrapped in a flannel shirt. One of his "clients" had been unable to pay him, and Troy had taken the pistol with him to settle the debt. The 15-year-old who'd given it to him had been found soon after to have a cache of homemade weapons. Luckily for Troy, the kid's arrest happened after Troy had acquired the gun. He'd figured it would come in handy one day.

That day had come. Will wasn't getting away with this. *No fuckin' way. He needs to learn a lesson. He can't treat me like that and get away with it.*

"Where the fuck is it?" he snarled.

As Troy tore through his closet, chucking things out one by one as he sought his redemption, he grabbed a large shoebox held together with a rubber band. When he caught sight of what was in his hand, he dropped the box and reflexively drew back, as if stung. The box fell on its side. The desiccated rubber band snapped off, and the contents spilled out. What Troy saw there froze him.

At his feet were the remnants of his life when his

mother was a part of it, his maternal memorabilia—
all that he had left of her. Slowly, he knelt down next
to the old birthday cards, the lock of hair held
together by a ponytail holder, a soft sweater she used
to wear. Shaking, he reached out to touch it. And was
lost.

Chapter Twenty

Will drove aimlessly for a while, churning the conversation he'd had with Troy over and over in his mind.

What the fuck? he thought. *What colossal balls! He's blaming* me *for this*! Hot anger coursed through him. But underneath, Will was perplexed and hurt. After all, he thought of Troy as his adopted little brother. It helped Will to have Troy to pal around with and to look after. It eased the pain of his brother's death and the empty aftermath. Will had so wholeheartedly embraced Troy that he had overlooked Troy's involvement in what had to have been small drug transactions.

I guess I did *know*, Will admitted to himself. *I knew he was selling grass, but a lot of kids smoke it.*

Will himself refrained from using pot, alcohol, or anything stronger because he was a dedicated athlete. He also didn't like the way drinking made him feel out of control, so he was cool with being the designated driver if his friends wanted to party on the weekend. Weed wasn't a big deal—so what if Troy and his other little friends smoked a little?

But Troy's attitude had really thrown him off. He'd thought they were brothers, and brothers stick together. Now Troy was calling him a narc, and that was *after* Troy had lied to the cops about Will. Was he being a sucker? Was Troy using him?

Thoughts bludgeoned Will's mind. He pictured himself in jail, sleeping on a hard bed, using a communal toilet, eating bologna on white bread.

Don't go there, don't go there.

What could he do? Could Declan get him out of this mess? What about Troy? Why the fuck did Troy throw him under the bus?

I know he's got problems, but look at his family. They're a mess. No wonder he has issues, Will thought. *I'm older than he is, and I have a great dad. Troy needs help. Maybe I'll figure out a way to help the little punk even if he thinks he doesn't need it. But first that little fucker's gonna have to set the record straight.*

Nodding to himself, Will decided to go over to the park, shoot some baskets, and blow off some steam.

Chapter Twenty-One

Troy was still on the floor of his bedroom, immersed in his little-boy memories, grieving inside for the mother who had thrown him away like an empty milk carton. He stared down at the little photo album that held the only pictures he had left of her. He'd hidden it from his father, who, in a drunken rampage, had gotten rid of every picture and personal effect she had left behind. He'd nearly set the house on fire, piling up pictures and cards and clothing in the fire pit and setting them ablaze. If he hadn't secreted the pictures he and his mom had taken in a photo booth at the Ocean Beach Boardwalk, his father would have torched them as well.

Troy gazed upon his mother's celluloid face as his heart twisted. He wanted to blame her, but he couldn't. It was his own fault. He was unlovable. He secretly worshiped and longed for his mother, and at that moment felt absolutely destitute without her.

So vulnerable.

It was the worst time to have his seller come to collect on his debt. Because Troy didn't have the money, either. Ryan Sullivan hadn't been the only client who'd been unable to pay him this week. Now Troy was left holding the bag.

Without warning, Troy's dealer and two thugs banged through the front door and stomped into Troy's room. Startled, Troy dropped the photo album and tried to sweep it out of sight.

But Guzman, the dealer, had quick eyes. He had to, in this business.

"Hey there, Sweet Cheeks," he said in a soft voice that belied the menace behind them. "Papa's come to collect his greenbacks. You got 'em all for me this time?"

Troy was usually pretty timely with his payments, but his clientele—largely high school students, and even middle schoolers—were not so reliable.

"Uh, hey, Guzman, how're you?" Troy said as he stood and brushed off his hands. "I wasn't expecting you."

"I can see that," he said. "Whatcha got there?" he asked, reaching for the photo album.

Panicked, Troy grabbed it away. "Nothing."

Guzman's phony smile slid off his face.

"Maybe I wanna see it anyway." He grabbed the album and flipped through it.

"Wow, she's hot." His glance flicked up at Troy. "Who's that? Your mom? I'd do her." He laughed.

Troy lunged at him.

The two enforcers jumped on him, and Troy went down. While one thug held Troy's head to the floor with a knee, Guzman bent down close to Troy's face.

"Oh, Troy, you got a anger problem. Don't you remember who I am?"

Troy grunted.

"I'm the guy you don't fuck with. Now, I need my money. Where is it?"

"I don't have it all," Troy managed.

More pressure from the knee to the head. Sweat started rolling down Troy's face, stinging his eyes.

"Where is it? What'd you do with it?" Guzman swooped back down and stuck a finger in Troy's face. "You been using the product yourself?"

"No, no, no. I have most of the money, but some guy stole the rest. A guy who I thought was my friend. He's kinda big and he's stronger than I am. A basketball player. I couldn't get the money back. I was just about to go over to his house with my gun and get the rest of the cash."

"Oooh, you got a gun, huh? Well, we'll take care of your client this time, okay? What's this kid's name? Where can I find him?"

"Will. Will Van Dalen."

Chapter Twenty-Two

It hadn't taken much persuasion for Troy to divulge Will's likely whereabouts.

Apparently, thought Guzman, *Will likes to play basketball, rain or shine, happy or sad, good days and bad. That's his drug, man, the basketball court. That's what he shoots.* Guzman chuckled to himself. *Not for long, though, unless he still has the cash.*

The sun was a red ball behind the trees as the crew drove past Grant Street Park. Will announced his presence even before they caught sight of him with the *bounce bounce bounce* of the basketball on the pavement and then the *bang!* on the backboard. Guzman sat in the back seat, devising a plan. He wanted to make it quick and painful, the way consequences should be.

Guzman had Enforcer #2, Enrique, put Step One into play. Ricky was small and looked relatively harmless. Guzman had chosen him for that very reason. When they pulled up at the park, Ricky hopped out and went up to the basketball court.

Ricky waved at Will and put his hand up to catch the ball. Will reacted out of habit and passed the ball to Ricky.

"Hey, man, you wanna get a game together?" Ricky bounced the ball and shot the ball. The ball thunked off the backboard, missing the basket altogether.

"It's gettin' a little late," Will said. "Besides," he added, eyeing the car, "we don't have enough guys."

"Ah, it's just for fun. Shoot a few baskets. Whaddya say?" asked Ricky.

"Sure, sure, okay," answered Will, his good-naturedness coming into play despite his initial wariness. He was kind of starved for competition, anyway.

Ricky came over to give him a high five. As Will put his arm up, Ricky caught Will's right wrist in his left hand and bent Will's right hand back hard and fast, almost snapping the bone. Will cried out and dropped to his knees on the court.

"Where's the money, motherfucker?" Ricky demanded.

"What money? What're you talking about?" Will tried to focus on what was happening. The throbbing pain in his wrist and up his arm was making it difficult.

"Troy's money, man," he said as he continued to twist Will's wrist. "You stole Troy's money, and he owes that to us. Where is it?"

"I didn't steal Troy's money," Will protested. "That's bullshit."

Ricky let go of Will's wrist, grabbed a blackjack from his back pocket, and rendered a savage blow to the side of Will's head. Will collapsed on the court.

After Ricky searched Will's pockets, he hightailed it back to the car and hopped in.

"Let's get outta here," he said.

"What the hell happened?" Guzman asked.

"Claims he didn't have the money, even after I bent his wrist and dropped him to the ground. I put him to sleep for a while. Nothing in his pockets, either."

"Shit."

Chapter Twenty-Three

Troy was nursing a headache while listlessly sorting through the items in his shoebox. Old lip gloss, the print on the plastic worn away by handling. His mother used it. Years ago. Troy rubbed it like a talisman or an ancient lamp that could grant him three wishes. He stared vacantly across his room as he fought off waves of guilt. Troy didn't do guilt. Not well, anyway. He was mostly angry. He preferred anger. Angry at his mom for leaving him behind. Angry at his father for not being enough for her. Angry at himself on some level for being disposable. For his inability to fulfill his mother's needs. *Why couldn't she love me?*

But he couldn't articulate any of this. It was too painful, too threatening. He desperately wanted a different subject to dwell upon. The most obvious was the trouble he was in and how he'd transferred it to Will. He looked into the shoebox and sifted around for more comfort.

Chapter Twenty-Four

Pain coursed through Will's head. It felt as if a shrieking noise were cleaving his skull in two. That pain vied with the throbbing in his wrist.

Where am I? he wondered before blackness washed over him once again.

After screaming north at a speed well beyond the posted limit, the red-and-white ambulance arrived at Jersey Shore University Hospital's Emergency Room dock, lights flashing. The team swiftly rolled the still-unconscious Will into the ER proper, where a nurse waited. A team rushed Will into the depths of the hospital for a CT scan, X-ray, and bloodwork to determine the extent of his injuries.

Awareness dawned again for Will. Bright lights stabbed his eyes, intensifying the pain in his head and wrist. He was vaguely aware of voices around him— *what are they saying?* He couldn't make it out, something about his head. Also, a sensation of being hoisted from one place to a hard table. Then…

shuddering motion and a breeze blowing across his body… that felt good, at least…

Chapter Twenty-Five

W*hat else could go wrong?* Bill wondered as he sat in the ER sitting area, waiting for news of Will's condition. The downward spiral had started two years earlier, when Carolyn and Patrick had been killed. That event had set in motion a whirlpool that had been sucking the life and energy from him since. Every day was a fight through invisible quicksand.

Yes, his business had suffered. He couldn't seem to keep his mind on the details. It had once been second nature but had flipped overnight to a continuous battle. That was bad enough, but he was fighting an internal war too—one of negative thoughts and self-loathing for failing Carolyn, for failing Patrick. Thoughts like these were a constant distraction.

People had been understanding for a while. But memories are short and forgiveness has its limits. Customers expected prompt responses, crisp attention, and loads of satisfaction. Bill's employees were loyal, but they often felt the heat. They had been afraid to approach Bill—after all, how much could a man take?

After the initial trauma of Carolyn and Patrick's deaths, the workers tried to protect him. But when his distractedness began to lose them major accounts, the troops started to worry, and the lumber manager, Gary Newscomb, had to address it.

Bill recalled the day when Gary appeared in his office doorway, paper in hand, looking pale and worried. Bill hadn't noticed at first. He was staring off into space. He looked up in surprise when Gary cleared his throat.

"Oh, Gary. Sorry, I didn't see you there." He blushed, embarrassed to be caught daydreaming.

"No problem, boss." Gary entered but remained standing, looking ill at ease. "Uh, sorry to bother you, but I thought you needed to see this." Gary handed over the paper he was holding. It turned out to be a letter from one of the Harrington-Davis Group.

Bill quickly scanned the letter, a diatribe from Robert Harrington. Years ago, Bill had landed the Harrington-Davis lumber contract, a virtual fortune-maker, since Harrington-Davis was the third-largest home builder in the state of New Jersey. In recent years, they had branched out into neighboring states, and the income from that business supplied about forty percent of Bill's trade. Bill and Robert had enjoyed a collegial relationship for years. The tone of this letter, however, made the pit of Bill's stomach drop. He could hardly believe what he was reading.

A great buzzing noise sounded in his head, and his palms became damp.

He put his hand to his head. "How can this be happening?" he all but whispered.

The letter read, in part:

Dear Mr. Van Dalen:

So formal, thought Bill. *Why this shift?*

For some time now, the attention to detail and prompt response to inquiries and orders I and my company once received by yours has been lacking. Despite multiple attempts to resolve these problems, they continue and have been affecting our ability to meet deadlines. The situation has threatened both our business and our reputation. Therefore, please be advised that I am exercising our right to withdraw from our contract. Given the congenial nature of our previous relationship, I have chosen to inform you personally rather than involve our respective attorneys. However, should you decide to contest this matter, please understand that I will have no other option than to turn this over to legal counsel. I regret that it has come to this. As of the 31st of this month, Harrington-Davis will be severing its contract with your company, Van Dalen Lumber & Landscaping.

Bill felt a wave of cold fear wash over him, and he was hit with a sudden surge of nausea. *Can this really be happening?* he thought. *Have I been that out of touch? Good Lord, make it stop.* He bent his head over his desk.

"Boss, are you ok?"

Bill had completely forgotten Gary's presence. He swallowed, squeezed the corners of his eyes, and plastered what he hoped was a confident expression onto his face.

"Fine, fine, Gary."

He doesn't look so fine, Gary thought. *Neither does Van Dalen Lumber & Landscaping.* But he kept his thoughts to himself. After all, he had been with the company for twenty years, since the very beginning, and he wasn't a young man. He had hoped to retire from this job.

"We'll weather this storm," Bill continued. "Just like we weathered everything else."

God, I hope not, thought Gary. They hadn't been weathering anything well at all since Mrs. Van Dalen and Patrick had been crushed by that train.

"Is there anything I can do, Bill?" Gary asked, only to be interrupted by the phone on Bill's desk.

Bill managed a sickly smile in Gary's direction. "I'll let you know. Thanks, Gary." Bill nodded his head in dismissal.

Now here he was, in the hospital, his only son

undergoing treatment. The pieces of Bill's life were whirling out of control. He'd already been late with a mortgage payment this year. Now he was facing bankruptcy. Worse still, as if everything that had happened to Will in the last 48 hours weren't enough, Will had been found unconscious in the park by a couple of teenagers. He had a head wound, and his condition was as yet undetermined, or at least hadn't been reported to Bill. Bill's mind was a mess of random, panicked thoughts. Everything seemed to be chained together in a vortex that was sucking him under. Overwhelmed by despair, Bill put his head into his hands.

Chapter Twenty-Six

By eight-thirty that evening, at least one of Bill's dire worries was put to rest. Dr. Patel, an ER physician, had asked Bill to join him inside Will's curtained cubicle.

Will was sitting up on the bed, putting on his sneakers.

"He sustained a blow to the head and had to get a few stitches," said Dr. Patel. "His memory and concentration may be a little foggy. That's completely normal. He can resume his normal activities as he feels up to it. He should see his family doctor in about 10 to 14 days to have the stitches removed." Dr. Patel closed Will's chart.

Bill was confused. "Okay, but what happened? What blow to the head?" He turned to Will. "Were you playing basketball when this happened?"

Will glanced at Dr. Patel, who gazed steadily back at him.

"I can't remember exactly what happened," Will said, unconsciously bringing his hand up to his head where he'd been struck by Ricky's blackjack.

"I keep remembering bits and pieces, but they don't make sense."

Bill looked to Dr. Patel for help.

"It's best to go home and rest for now," Dr. Patel said reassuringly. "I'm sure your memory will return." He looked at Will again. "You take care of yourself, Will."

Will shook hands with the doctor and walked out with his father.

It worried Bill that his son had little memory of why he had collapsed on the court, but he decided to let it go, for now. He had enough on his mind, and badgering Will with questions might only worsen his condition.

Chapter Twenty-Seven

W ill awoke on Wednesday morning aware that the sun was shining, even though his eyes were still shut. *If the sun is shining, then why do I feel like crap?* Will wondered. *Oh. I'm still suspended. And I have stitches in my head.* He sighed.

He hardly recognized his life. He wasn't sure where to begin or what to do about any of it. Not only was he suspended and home with a head injury, but a school project loomed before him like a brick wall. *All right,* he thought. *What was the way Coach had taught the team to attack the adversary? Head straight for the thing you're most scared of, and you're likely to find it wasn't as powerful as you thought.*

It was the same if you got into a street fight, Will thought, still lying in his bed but now, with his eyes open. *If you attack the biggest guy and knock him down, nobody else will mess with you.*

He had a flash of memory: a guy coming up to him on the basketball court. A guy he didn't know.

Just as quickly, it disappeared. Will sighed. *I'd better deal with the things I can focus on.*

Judy had told him a story that had the same underlying philosophy. It was called "Run to the Roar" and had been used by Paul Assaiante, the squash and tennis coach at Trinity College, who had been dubbed the "winningest coach" in history. The idea, Judy had explained in one of his sessions when he was grappling with latent fears following his mother's and brother's deaths, is drawn from the way that lions hunt their prey. In reality, female lions do the hunting, but they use the large, old, toothless male lion, which still looks and sounds plenty scary, to frighten the prey right into the jaws of the lionesses. The lionesses gather, hidden, on one side of the intended prey. Then, from the other direction, the male advances upon the prey and roars his loudest roar. The prey, startled and terrified, runs in the opposite direction—headlong to its death.

Will threw back the covers and jumped up out of bed, ready to at least *try* to figure out a way to attack his project and win. He felt the *thud!* of his feet hitting the ground all the way in his head. *Whoa, boy! Okay, maybe I gotta go a little slower this morning.*

Half an hour later, Will had thrown on a pair of jeans and a sweatshirt and had breakfasted like a king on a bowl of cereal. He had texted a few of his teammates to see whether they would meet him the next day after practice to shoot the shit. Then he pulled out his project outline, his notebook, a pad, and got to work. Despite a headache, he was determined to run to the roar.

He first looked at the project outline. *Okay,* he thought. *I know I have to analyze the interactions of the three main characters, but how do I do that?* Will sat there for a minute, distracted by an itching ankle. He scratched it, but it continued to itch. He scratched it again. *Damn socks,* he thought. He wiggled around in his chair, trying to get comfortable. He'd found his jeans in the dryer, and they were a little tight. He wiggled a little more, then determinedly reread the outline.

How'm I gonna analyze the social interactions of these people? he wondered. *Maybe I should look at what social interactions they had. Yeah, that's a good idea!* he thought, giving himself mental encouragement and feeling a lightning surge of satisfaction at having arrived at a direction. He leaped to his feet, grabbed his book bag, and began searching through it for the notes he had taken while reading the book.

Of course, the notes weren't in the book bag because when Will had gotten frustrated yesterday he had dumped everything out and hadn't yet thought about putting it back. He looked around the room for his notebook but all he could see was his unmade bed, so, without really thinking about priorities, he began to wrestle with the sheets and blankets.

Once the bed was made—however haphazardly—Will stepped back to admire his handiwork. His gaze fell on his desk and he realized that he had been in the middle of searching for his notes. *Right,* he thought. *I'm not getting a prize for being the most organized guy in class.*

Will resumed his search. He got down on his knees and lifted up the edge of the comforter, which was obscuring his view of whatever was underneath his bed. It was kind of dim under there, though, and he couldn't see very well, so he stuck his head under the bed frame. Nothing much under the bed except some old socks and some dust bunnies.

Will sat back on his heels and scanned his room. He stood up, went to the end of the bed, and moved it away from the wall. *Aha!* he thought. The missing notebook had slid between the bed and the wall. He retrieved it and sat back down at the desk. *Okay, where was I? Oh, yeah. I have to look at what social interactions the characters had.*

He scanned his notes, looking for evidence of social interactions. As he gazed down at the words he'd written, however, his mind began to wander. He found himself remembering the scene in his own car last Sunday night. He could hear Troy yelling, *"Where's my money?"* and Ryan's terrified voice responding, *"I'm sorry! Troy, I'm sorry! Please don't kill me!"* He remembered looking into the rearview mirror and seeing Troy holding a knife to Ryan's throat. Again, he saw Ryan's eyes popping out of his head.

Catching himself, Will shook his head and put his face in his hands. "I gotta stop thinking about this," he said to himself.

Sighing, he returned to his notes. "Maybe if I read out loud, I won't start daydreaming," he said to himself. "Okay, who's doing what here?"

Will spent a couple of hours reviewing his notes and taking new notes about social interactions between the characters on a separate sheet of paper. He took a break for lunch, then went back to work. He kept checking his cell phone, but none of his teammates had texted him back.

Weird, he thought. *Maybe they're too busy with school and practice today.* But he didn't quite believe that, and began to feel disheartened.

By the middle of the afternoon, Will had made pages of notes with as many social interactions as he could think of between the characters of the film. Now he had to organize them. Just the thought of it made him want to close the books and go do something else. He had a pounding headache to boot.

But Will hadn't been in counseling for so long without having learned something. He knew he was trying to avoid his issues, which included a long-standing difficulty staying focused. *Okay,* Will thought. *Great. I know I'm supposed to do something different here, but what?*

He racked his brain. *Maybe it's HALT. Hungry, angry, lonely, tired. Am I hungry? No. Am I angry? Yes. I'm angry at Troy. I'm angry at the police for thinking I did something wrong. I'm angry at Mr. Anderson for suspending me when I didn't do anything wrong. Am I lonely? Yeah, maybe a little,* he admitted. *I haven't seen my friends or been to practice and nothing feels* normal. *Am I tired? No.*

Okay, he continued thinking the way he'd been taught to. *So I'm angry and I'm lonely. How do I change that? I already told Troy off. I can talk about the anger with Judy tomorrow. I could go talk to the police, but they don't give a shit. And I'm not allowed on school property while I'm suspended. So that about covers the anger. How about the lonely? Maybe I can find some of the guys later and hang out.*

Marginally cheered that he had at least figured out what was bugging him, he decided to reward himself by closing his books for the day, never realizing that he had successfully avoided the real problem: how to begin organizing the material for his paper.

Bill came home at quarter to five to pick Will up for their appointment with Declan. He surprised Will, who had gotten caught up in playing video games and completely forgotten about the meeting.

When Bill called him, Will jumped up, turned off his computer, and galloped down the stairs.

"Let's go," said Bill, and they were out the door and on their way.

Declan Fennelly's office was on Arnold Avenue in a stately building that dated back to the early part of the 20th century. He was a solo practitioner and had only one employee: his secretary, Arlene. He always joked that Arlene didn't need him; she could run the office perfectly well without him. Even if he were away on vacation or had ended up in the hospital, no one would know he was missing if Arlene was at the helm. Brisk and cheerful, she displayed a constant smile and kept her blond hair short—an altogether pleasant woman in her early sixties.

It was Arlene who greeted Bill and Will when they entered the office. She asked them to have a seat in the waiting area. Will wore his customary jeans and long-sleeved T-shirt with his letter jacket. Bill still wore his work "uniform" of business slacks, button-down shirt, and loafers. They had barely seated themselves before Arlene returned, smiling as usual, and informed them that Mr. Fennelly was ready to see them.

After brief handshakes and a nod from Declan, everyone took his seat.

Even though the situation would have caused

anxiety in most people, Will wasn't nervous. He had known Declan Fennelly all his life, and he had unquestioning faith that Mr. Fennelly would solve this problem. Besides, his predicament still felt like more of an "adult" issue. If anything, Will was curious as to how his dad and Mr. Fennelly would go about it, though he was sure they had a few tricks up their sleeves. So it was with some surprise that Will saw Mr. Fennelly present the situation in a very concerned manner.

Unlike Arlene, Declan wasn't smiling. He sat back in his chair with his hands clasped across his abdomen and surveyed father and son.

Declan Fennelly had watched Will grow up. He had been present at all Will's birthday parties and had taken Will fishing more than once. Will had sometimes come to him for advice, including when his mother was in the hospital on life support. Declan had offered the boy male comfort and a shoulder to cry on since Bill was still numb from trying to deal with the whole situation. It was with some trepidation, then, that the attorney faced father and son across his desk. His unease lay in the nature of the charges, the publicity they had garnered, and the current political climate. Legally, Will was an adult. He was involved in an alleged kidnapping and assault with a deadly weapon on a minor. He would face jail time if he was convicted. Declan had reviewed the documents he'd gotten from the prosecutor's office, including the witness statements. He believed he could get a dismissal of the charges or obtain a pretrial settlement agreement if the right assistant prosecutor was assigned to the case. That was pure luck, however, and Declan didn't like leaving things to chance. Most of the APs were decent attorneys just doing their job. They'd see right off the bat that Will was not a menace to society. But there were a few rabid, self-righteous pricks in the prosecutor's office, and that could pose a real problem. Will was not the kind of young man who could do time and come away unscathed. For those reasons, Declan planned to prepare Bill and Will for the worst-case scenario.

The pretrial intervention program was intended to provide relief to both the court system and to the first-time offender. It saved the resources of the judiciary for serious cases and it gave a second chance to someone like Will, who might have simply made a bad decision without criminal intent. If Declan obtained PTI for Will, Will could have his criminal proceedings postponed for up to three years. At the conclusion of the agreed-upon time period, the judge could dispose of the case in various ways, including a complete dismissal of the charges.

Declan explained all this to Bill and Will in as gentle and straightforward a manner as he could. He advised father and son that, under the circumstances, it might be wise to negotiate the best outcome they could without going to trial. That would allow Will to resume his position on the basketball team as soon as the ink was dry on the settlement agreement. If the case went to trial, it could take months, if not years, to conclude. That choice would be extremely important for Will's future.

"Why not go to trial?" Bill asked.

"There's a rule in the law: a settled case is a better case. That's because, when you settle, you have some control over the outcome. If the case goes to trial, no matter how well you prepare the evidence and the witnesses, anything can happen. Witnesses mix up their stories, blurt out things they never told you. Juries can make wild decisions. Judges can rule against us."

Declan continued the meeting with a discussion of the charges against Will. He explained that, in New Jersey, there are two kinds of assault: simple and aggravated. "A person is guilty of assault," explained Declan, "if he tries to cause or actually causes bodily injury to another person. You'd be guilty of assault even if you just physically menaced them so they are in fear of 'imminent serious bodily injury.' So, the act of confining a person in a car and threatening them with a knife would qualify as assault."

"But Mr. Fennelly, I didn't hold the knife to Ryan's throat."

Declan held up a forefinger. "When a lawyer is

interpreting a statute for a client or for the court, there is a rule of thumb that we follow: 'Read on, read on, read on.' It means that you have to look at *all* of the law and take it into consideration. Hear me out."

Will settled back in his seat.

"Simple assault is a disorderly person's offense. While it's not really a crime, it is considered a violation of law and can result in a criminal conviction and a criminal record. Aggravated assault is more serious. It consists of attempts to cause serious bodily injury to another or attempts to cause bodily injury with a deadly weapon—like a knife."

As he was talking, Declan's eyes roved back and forth between Bill and Will. Will stared back as if hypnotized, his mouth hanging slightly open in a posture of disbelief, as if he had been suddenly and unexpectedly struck by a cosmic force of unknown origin. Bill, on the other hand, listened intently, his face pale, his body still except for his index fingers, which pressed down hard on the cuticles of his thumbs, his fingernails tearing at the tender skin.

Declan continued. "Kidnapping is when one person holds another as a hostage with the purpose of holding him for ransom or reward." Declan saw Will's eyebrows rise, but the boy remained silent. "Kidnapping can also mean holding another to facilitate the commission of a crime or to inflict bodily injury on another, or to terrorize the victim. Kidnapping is a crime of the first degree and, in New Jersey, can carry a sentence of between 15 and 30 years."

Will's eyes grew even bigger.

"However, if the actor releases the victim unharmed and in a safe place prior to apprehension, the crime is reduced to a second-degree crime.

"Now we come to the interesting part." He looked Will in the eye. "You've also been charged with conspiracy. To be guilty of conspiracy, all you need do is agree with another person that at least one of you will commit a crime. You would also be guilty of conspiracy if you agreed to help another person to plan or commit a crime, or to even attempt to commit a crime."

The expression on Will's face indicated that he was hopelessly lost.

"I know I'm throwing a lot at you guys," said Declan as he caught Bill's expression of controlled panic. "Let's talk about how what happened on Sunday night fits these different charges."

Bill continued to gaze steadily at Declan, his head slanted down, his eyes peering up from under his eyebrows. He remained perfectly still, waiting. At that moment, the grandfather clock in the waiting room chimed out the quarter hour. The elegant tone of the chime now sounded foreboding, like the gonging of the clock in Charles Dickens' *A Christmas Carol* heralding the arrival of the spirits.

Declan continued, "The pertinent facts in your case are these: 16-year-old Troy calls and asks you to pick him up. Eighteen-year-old-adult you goes willingly. At the pizza parlor, Troy tells you he has to swing by Ryan Sullivan's house. He tells you Ryan owes him some money. For what, he doesn't say, but deep down inside, you know. You drive over to Ryan's and Troy tells him to hop in the backseat. Troy tells you to take off, drive over to the park. You drive away and the car doors lock. Now 15-year-old Ryan is stuck in the back with 18-year-old you at the wheel. Then Troy jumps back there and menaces him with a switchblade, scaring the daylights out of the kid, making him plead for his life. He thinks Troy's going to kill him. This is all over money that Ryan owes Troy for a controlled substance."

Declan paused, looking back and forth between the two faces staring back at him. He saw the keen understanding in Bill's eyes that the circumstances of the situation looked bad for Will and that the outcome could be dire. Will's eyes, however, still had that vacant look. "Are you getting the picture?"

"When you put it like that," Will said, "it sounds terrible."

Declan had been leaning back in his burgundy leather chair with his ankle on his knee, swiveling a little from side to side. He stopped. "You're right,

Will, it does sound terrible. And it'll sound even worse if the matter goes to trial. The prosecutor will make you look like the latest scourge to hit the Jersey Shore, as if you planned to murder Ryan."

At that point, Bill sat upright in his chair and jumped into the conversation. "Okay, Declan, I think we get that these charges against Will are much more serious than we first understood when this all started." Bill's face was creased with the strain of keeping his emotions in check. "But what's the best course of action?

Bill's questions charged the air with an electric quality, but Declan, deliberately leaning back in his chair to project an air of calm, steepled his hands in front of his chest and once more crossed his ankle over his knee.

This was a chess game for Declan—albeit one with dire consequences for his godson if he lost— and he had to think ahead to the moves he was going to make to win. "Here's what we're going to do..."

Declan proceeded to outline the steps he could take to oppose the charges against Will, all the way from calling the prosecutor and speaking to her informally to filing a motion to dismiss for lack of evidence against Will. Even though it was Troy who had perpetrated the crime, Will looked better in the media: he was an adult and the captain of the basketball team. It made good media coverage, especially during an election year.

"The path of least resistance—and the least expensive—might be to try for pretrial intervention," said Declan.

"What's that?" asked Bill.

"PTI is like putting the case on hold for a period of time for up to three years. You'd enter a contract with the prosecutor's office. In a way, it's like being on probation. There'd be periodic check-ins and possibly other requirements, like some community service. If you attend school, continue with counseling, and stay out of trouble, there should be no problem. We'd need the recommendation of the county criminal division manager and the consent of the prosecutor, though."

Bill looked discouraged. "How likely is it that we'll get it in an election year?"

"Will's got as good a shot as anyone," said Declan. "Even more so, because he's never had any police involvement or legal troubles before, he's captain of the basketball team, and his grades are decent. He's a good kid. If the prosecutor really wants justice to be served here, the outcome should not be for Will to go to jail."

At the mention of his grades, he felt a fresh wave of shame and self-loathing. This was a new experience for Will, and he didn't know how to cope with it. *I'm*

18 years old, but I still need my dad and Mr. Fennelly to bail me out. I'm the one who fucked this whole thing up. Now my dad's got to rescue me. I'm so stupid.

Bill was leaning forward in his chair with his forearms on his knees. "Would that be any better, though? I mean, if we put this thing on ice for three years, he'll be 21 years old, and wouldn't it be even worse to deal with it then? I mean, he'd be three years older, and no longer a teenager or a high school student."

"Bill, the goal is for the whole thing to just go away. If we get PTI, then Will's life gets to go back to normal. At the end of two or three years, he has to report back to the court. In between now and then, he goes to school, plays ball, and stays out of trouble, then goes to college and starts building his future. Down the road, the judge will see this whole incident for what it really is: Will was in the wrong place at the wrong time. Then we just get the charges dismissed and his record will be expunged."

Bill was looking at Declan with the first hopeful expression he'd worn during the whole consultation. "You mean it's just that easy?"

"It could be, Bill, but I can't promise you that. All I can promise is that we can try." Declan looked at Will. "Do you understand what we've been talking about, Will?"

"Yes, sir, I think so."

"I think we should try it," said Bill, straightening up. He glanced at Will. "How about it, Will?"

"If you think so, Dad. Yeah."

"So what happens in the meantime, Declan? Can we get Will back into school somehow?"

"Give me a coupla days, Bill. I know the principal at the high school. I'll give him a call again, and I'll get in touch with the prosecutor's office, find out who's handling the case, and see whether I can end this thing sooner rather than later."

Declan stood to signal that the consultation was over. He extended his hand and clasped Bill's tightly, putting his left hand on Bill's shoulder. "I'll give you a call just as soon as I know something. Until then, you leave everything to me, including the worrying."

Declan turned and shook Will's hand. "You take care now, Will. Don't worry. I'll take care of this." Secretly, he hoped he'd be able to deliver on his promise.

Chapter Twenty-Eight

After the session with Declan, Bill felt almost buoyant as he and Will walked to the Tahoe. In fact, he felt like celebrating.

He turned to Will, grinning as he hadn't all week. "How about we go to Joey's for a burger?"

Catching his father's mood, Will grinned back. "Sure, Dad, I'm suddenly starved."

Father and son hopped into the car and drove the short distance to Joey's Bar & Grill on Route 209 South. They pulled into the city parking lot across the street, which served the businesses on both Route 209 and Main Street, which bisected the highway just south of Joey's. After parking the Tahoe, they hoofed it across the road, and pulled on a brass handle to open Joey's wood-and-frosted-glass door.

The mood inside Joey's seemed to match their own: the bar area, where they entered, was standing room only, the football game was in full swing on huge screens mounted around the room, and the crowd raised a happy din, jostling for space and attention, swilling draft beer and eating peanuts.

Bill and Will were shown to a table in the adjoining area, which was a square room, elevated by about a foot, to the left of the bar. The tin ceiling, corner fireplace, trailing greenery, and brass accents made for a cozy atmosphere.

After glancing at the menu, both men ordered their favorite, a bacon cheeseburger. Joey's was famous for its 10-ounce sirloin burgers, guaranteed not to disappoint. As they sipped their beverages, waiting for the food to arrive, Bill noticed a few glances in their direction the bar area. One after another, faces turned their way, heads bent, and voices whispered. Although he began to grow uncomfortable, he was determined that Will not notice. He gave a silent thanks that Will was facing in the opposite direction.

When the food arrived, Will dug in with gusto and Bill gave it his best, although by now even the noise level in the bar had diminished from its earlier volume. Will, however, was talking happily about getting back to basketball practice.

By the time Bill was looking over the check and digging out his wallet, the level of conversation in the bar had dropped noticeably, and patrons were glancing at him and Will. It made Bill uncomfortable, and he was eager to leave. Just when he thought they would escape, a man left the bar and headed toward their table. Standing about six feet four and weighing at least two-forty, the guy was imposing. As he drew closer, he caught Bill's eye, but didn't smile. Planting his hands on his hips, he launched into a speech that made Will's head snap to attention.

Without preamble or greeting, he said, "You may have noticed that it's gotten quiet in here since you came in. None of us are happy to see you and your son in here after what he did to Ryan Sullivan, and we wanted you to know." He glanced at Will and said, "Maybe you should pick on someone your own size."

Will's mouth hung open, and Bill was stunned into momentary silence. Feeling the need to defend his son and to correct the injustice that had been done to him, Bill sat back in his chair and said, in deliberately measured tones, "My name is Bill Van Dalen and I own a business in this town. I've lived here all my life. I'm not happy about what happened to Ryan Sullivan, but I'm far less happy that folks are jumping to conclusions about Will, and that's simply not fair to him. He's done nothing wrong, despite the rumors that some people are spreading." Bill looked pointedly into the man's eyes. "Will's a good student, captain of the basketball team, and he's the reason that Ryan didn't get hurt on Sunday night. He saved Ryan." Bill risked a glance around the now-hushed restaurant and bar. Then he looked back at the man in front of him. "If you really don't want to see young people get hurt, you should really get your facts straight before you make a public spectacle of yourself."

The man's eyes narrowed. "Are you calling me a liar?"

Bill felt his patience wearing thin. "No, sir, I'm not. But I have a son who has been wronged, just like Ryan Sullivan." Bill looked at Will as he rose to his feet. "Will, I think it's time we went on home." Stepping past the man, he grasped Will's left bicep and steered him out of the restaurant.

The cool, sea-scented air was bracing. Wired from the confrontation, Bill hustled Will across the street toward the Tahoe and headed home. As they drove farther and farther from the restaurant, the tension subsided and Bill's muscles uncoiled, leaving him flat and somewhat nauseous.

Bill stole a glance at Will's face, which was illuminated by the glow of the dashboard lights. What he saw wrenched his heart. Will was staring straight ahead, eyes unfocused, face pale, as if he were a million miles away inside his own head.

"Will, are you okay? That guy was a complete ass. I'm sorry you were exposed to it."

"No, Dad, it's okay," said Will. "He's right. I'm not welcome anymore. Not in school, not on the basketball team, now not even in a bar."

"Will, that's not true! The basketball team is dying to get you back. Your absence has left a gaping hole. And as soon as Mr. Fennelly gets things straightened out with Mr. Anderson, you'll be back in school. You'll see. It'll all work out." He wanted to grab Will by the shoulders and break through the numbness in which he seemed to be encased. He was desperate that Will not sink into passive acceptance that the man at the bar represented the entirety of public opinion.

"Will, listen. We'll go home and get some rest. Things will look brighter in the morning. It's been a tough day." He glanced at Will's profile.

"Sure, Dad," Will answered, his gaze locked on the distant darkness.

Chapter Twenty-Nine

Declan Fennelly was as good as his word. Just after nine o'clock the next morning, he rang the high school and asked to speak to Joe Anderson. Joe was an old golf buddy and a fellow member of the local Rotary Club. Declan felt fairly certain that he could get Joe to help him return Will to school before the full term of his suspension was served. After all, he and Joe had worked hard together on various goodwill projects in the community, and he himself had done Joe a significant favor or two. In fact, the current potential for disaster in Will's life was similar to the time Joe got pulled over driving around in women's clothing on a Saturday night. Had Declan not intervened quickly in order to sanitize the incident and make it disappear, Joe's professional life would have been toast.

So, while he waited on hold for Joe, Declan had some confidence that, in this arena at least, he could get some immediate relief for Will. While he waited, Declan pondered the word "relief," a legal term.

Black's Law Dictionary defined it as the "redress or benefit that a party asks of a court." Of course, relief also meant "respite, reprieve, liberation, or assistance," which is exactly what Declan planned to get for Will through this phone conversation. The rest of Will's relief—his freedom and a clear record—would require Declan to show the court who Will really was and what had really happened that October evening.

Joe's abrupt greeting on the line startled Declan. "Declan, how are you? Long time, no see."

"Joe, my friend, you're absolutely right. My clients are keeping me busy these days. As a matter of fact, that's what I called you about. I've agreed to represent Will Van Dalen. I'm sure you heard about what happened. Or should I say, what *didn't* happen?"

There was a moment of silence on the other end. "Declan, you've got yourself a mess of a case in that one. You sure you want to take that on?"

"Bill's a long-time client and an old friend, and I happen to be Will's godfather, although my personal involvement with the family might be a good reason for me *not* to take the case." Declan gave a rueful half-grunt, half-laugh. "Anyway, Joe, I met with Will and his father last night, and we're going to seek pretrial intervention for Will. The reason I'm calling you this morning is to see how quickly we can get him back into school. I understand he's suspended, but can't we give him a week of detention or some kind of writing assignment so he can get back to school and play ball?"

Another pause on the line preceded Joe's measured response. "Declan, I don't think you understand the gravity of this situation. As a senior and captain of the basketball team, he has a certain public persona in this town, and this whole mess is squarely in the public eye. This *incident*," he gave the word a kind of sneering emphasis, "has been reported in the newspapers, on the local radio stations, and on television. I've had phone calls from CNN, ABC, CBS News, Channel 12—you name it. I've had phone calls from parents who are concerned about their students here. You'd think there was suddenly a rash of kidnappings around town."

When Declan began to respond, Joe interrupted him. "The worst phone calls, though, Declan, have been from the Board of Ed members. For better or worse—and I'll deny I ever said this—those folks are my boss. They've been getting a lot of public pressure, and they in turn have been pressuring me to expel Will from school."

Declan took a moment to digest this last bit of information. This conversation was going in exactly the opposite direction that he'd hoped it would. He felt as if he were being submerged under one of the Atlantic's waves. But Declan had years of legal training and experience, and although he did not relish what he had to do, he knew that he had to zealously represent his client. However, he also knew that another ethics rule—the prohibition on representing a client whose interests are directly adverse to another, or former, client's interest—would prevent him from acting on it. This was getting dicey.

"Joe," he said quietly. "I think you'll recall a time when you might have been in the middle of a mess that could have ended up squarely in the public eye, and I made sure it didn't." Declan let that sit a moment. He could hear Joe's breathing over the phone as he sat, stunned at the reminder of his own vulnerability.

"Now, Joe, I'm not saying that there's any chance that your own story would come out in connection with this. But think it over and ask yourself whether there's anything you can do for this kid. Will is the hero here. He saved Ryan Sullivan from that little shit, Troy Braithwaite. Troy is the bad actor here. Will is the good guy. He's a teenager, for Christ's sake, and he didn't do what he's accused of doing. This could ruin his whole life."

"Jesus Christ, Declan! What are you asking me to do here? The board's got a hold of this thing. They're not gonna listen to me. I'm telling you, the heat is on! We're living in a fishbowl here."

"Joe, Joe, calm down. I get it. I get it. Just see what you can do. There's got to be someone there who has some empathy for this kid. He's a good kid. See if you can put in a word for him with the right person, okay?"

"Okay, Declan, okay. I will. I understand. I'll try. But don't get your hopes up. You didn't hear these guys at the closed-session meeting."

"Joe, all I'm asking is that you do your best. See what you can do for Will and let me know, okay?"

"All right, Declan, I'll try."

"You try, Joe, and let me know, huh?"

After the call had ended, Declan let his head fall into his hands. He felt as if he had gravel in his stomach. *Litigation is a rough game*, he thought. *Not for those with a weak stomach.*

Chapter Thirty

By the end of third period, the quiet murmuring in class and in the hallways had broken down Troy's ability to focus. He had gotten through homeroom, World History, Spanish, and English on autopilot. His awareness had gradually increased until the switch flipped from internal to external focus, and he realized that he was drawing a lot more attention than usual. He began to return the other students' gazes, but they grew bolder.

As Troy walked down a hallway, Howie Mays, called out: "Hey, Troy, you know anything about what happened to Will Van Dalen at the park on Tuesday?'

Troy stopped. "Whadda you mean? What happened?"

"You mean you didn't hear?" Mays was skeptical, and Troy could hear it in his voice. A bad feeling washed over Troy.

"I'm asking, ain't I?" said Troy with more

courage than he felt.

Mays sauntered across the hall to face off with Troy. He stood for a moment, eyes traveling over Troy's face, as if searching for the truth, but not expecting to find it.

"Maybe you already know what happened," Mays said, his eyes a cold challenge.

"If I knew, would I be asking?"

"Good question, Braithwaite. In case you didn't hear, Will was pretty banged up when they brought him to the emergency room on Tuesday night."

Troy's eyes widened—in fear or surprise, Howie wasn't sure.

"No one knows what really happened. Two kids found Will lying on the basketball court, unconscious."

"Is he okay?" Troy asked, holding his breath.

"He got walloped in the head and they had to stitch him up. If you consider that okay, then I guess, yeah, he's okay. Except he's not okay; his life's a fuckin' mess."

At this point, Troy suddenly realized that he was surrounded by students who had moved even closer, hemming him in. He could feel them pressing in, and the air went out of his lungs and the space around him.

Howie looked down at Troy. "I'm wondering what happened to Will. I mean, he didn't fall down and get stitches all by himself."

Howie took a step closer to Troy.

Troy could feel his breath on his face. He said nothing, just stared into Howie's eyes as if they held him in some kind of a trance.

"I'm wondering who would beat Will up and leave him like that. I'm wondering who *could* beat him up and leave him like that. It's sort of odd that this happens right after he gets arrested for kidnapping and assaulting Ryan Sullivan." Howie's eyes took on a mean edge. "He doesn't even know Ryan Sullivan."

Howie took a step closer, and Troy stepped back inadvertently, right into the wall of students encircling him. He couldn't move. There was nowhere to go.

"But you do. Word going around," said Howie, "is that Ryan owes you some money. And that you used Will to scare him into paying you. I hope that's not true. 'Cuz if it is true…"

Just then, the fourth period bell rang. But Howie Mays had made his point. Troy's heart was pounding. He was trapped and wished that he were anywhere else but standing in that hallway, surrounded by Will's friends.

After a moment they drifted away, all of them

sending him looks of disdain, anger, and implied threat. It didn't take more than a heartbeat for Troy to decide that school was over for the day. He made for the nearest exit.

Chapter Thirty-One

On the other side of town, Bill became increasingly distracted as lunchtime drew near, imagining what might be happening between Declan Fennelly and Joe Andersen. *Was Declan in court this morning? Was Joe in school today? Maybe, even now, Joe was telling Coach Lichtenberg that Will would be permitted to return to school immediately. Or maybe Joe was calling the Board of Ed members one by one to determine where they stood on the issue, and no one was in favor of letting Will come back to school.*

Bill finally put his head in his hands as if to shut out these ungovernable thoughts.

"Stop! I have to stop thinking about it."

He put his pen down resolutely, stood up, and announced to his secretary, Ellen, he was going out for lunch. Although Bill scrupulously brought his lunch and always worked steadily through his lunch hour, Ellen was none too surprised that he was taking a break today.

"Looks like he's aged ten years in the past four days," she mumbled as he walked out the door. "And if I didn't know he's not a drinking man, I'd swear he had a hangover."

Shaking her head, she began cleaning up the mess Bill had made of his usually tidy desk. *It's all due to Will's foolishness*, she thought, straightening papers a little more vigorously than necessary. *It's about time he quit fooling around, got himself together and applied himself. His mother spoiled him, that's the problem. Fawning over that boy all the time.*

Ellen practically tsk-tsked out loud. She was more than a little sweet on Bill Van Dalen, however, and this had created a blind spot. She might criticize his son or his late wife, but he could do no wrong.

While Ellen made silent judgments and straightened up his desk, Bill strode aimlessly down the street. Gray and slate-blue clouds that predicted a storm obscured the sky, and the wind was as wild as his thoughts, whipping around from various directions and swirling the leaves in colorful eddies at his feet. He walked quickly, as if trying to elude the worries wormed unceasingly through his mind. *I've got to get a grip,* he thought, *or I'll never save my business. Maybe I should go and talk to Will's counselor myself.* He stopped abruptly. *I can't believe it's come to this. I've really got to get a grip.* Bill looked up and found himself standing in front of Jersey Mike's, a shop known for its submarine sandwiches. *Hungry, angry, lonely, tired,* he thought. *How about terrified and sad? It would still be first things first. I'm hungry and that means food.*

As Bill was ordering a turkey sub, Will was popping a package of frozen pizza snacks into the microwave. He was feeling dull and out of sort. He'd unwittingly contributed to this hangover malaise by sleeping late, then lying around playing video games.

As the microwave hummed, Will stared at the light and watched the pizza snacks riding around on a glass tray like dolls on a toy merry-go-round. He was mesmerized until the oven's bell sounded. He grabbed the snacks and flopped on the couch in front of the TV. The TV had been set to News 12 New Jersey. As Will focused in, he saw the reporter was standing near the train tracks.

"The police are investigating the death of a high school senior who was struck and killed by a southbound train on the North Jersey Coast Line just south of the Mantopan station," she said. "While neither the police nor the county prosecutor's office have commented, pending the outcome of the investigation, there is conjecture that the young man took his own life by walking onto the tracks last night."

Holy shit, thought Will. *That's the second one this week.* Will stared at the reporter talking into the camera. *What the hell is going on over there?*

Mantopan was only about one mile north of Ocean Beach. Then, after a moment, he thought: *Hah. Maybe he was falsely accused of a crime, arrested, and suspended all in the same 24 hours.*

Suddenly, the pizza snacks were unappealing, and the few that he'd already scarfed sat heavily in his stomach and felt vaguely nauseating. Will watched as the reporter interviewed some of the dead teen's friends and teachers. Then, the camera panned the area near the railroad tracks where police in uniform had gathered with men in suits wearing serious expressions. The interviews had a central theme: the dead student had everything to live for, and no one could believe he'd taken his own life. He was slated to go to college next year and had good prospects. Some thought there'd been an argument with his girlfriend just prior to the accident—if that's what it was—on the tracks. Others were concerned about the possibility of a suicide cluster—a social phenomenon in which one suicide triggers others within a small community.

"Wow," Will said. "He had way less reason to kill himself than I do. And I've never thought of doing that." *Till now*, he thought. Then he shook himself mentally and did a brief internal review. Despite the circumstances, Will had faith in Declan. *I've gotta get over this. I'm gonna be back in school soon, and what am I gonna look like at practice?*

Aiming the remote at the TV, Will shut it off and returned his plate to the kitchen, dumping the leftover pizza snacks in the garbage and stowing his plate in the dishwasher.

"Time to hit the books," he said, and jogged up the stairs.

Chapter Thirty-Two

Joe Anderson was still unnerved by his phone conference with Declan Fennelly. What the hell did he mean by suggesting that my story might come out? How the hell can that be related to Will Van Dalen? Is Declan threatening me? He can't be. He's a lawyer. He has ethical rules he has to follow.

Joe was still unsettled and tried to focus on what Declan had asked of him: Just see what you can do. There's got to be someone there who has some empathy for this kid. He's a good kid. See if you can put in a word for him with the right person, okay?

See what I can do? thought Joe. What can I do? Find someone who has empathy for Will Van Dalen? Good luck. Will might have been in the wrong place at the wrong time, but public sentiment in Ocean Beach is against him. He's 18 years old, for Christ's sake. How could he not know what he was doing, getting mixed up with the Braithwaite kid? No, there was no way he was completely innocent. He must have had them all fooled. Still, I did agree to try and put in a good word for him. With the right person.

Joe sighed and got heavily to his feet. He felt his mission was doomed from the beginning as he made his way across the central administration area to the superintendent's office. The superintendent—his boss—Vincent Flowers, was a man who loved to hear himself talk and loved even better to gaze at himself in the mirror and admire his hairstyle, custom-fitted suits, monogrammed shirts, and gold cuff links. Joe dreaded this encounter.

He knocked on the superintendent's door and was summoned into the inner sanctum. There sat the super, resplendent in a shirt with a freshly starched collar, pinstripes, and gold winking at all the masculine style points: tie bar, cuff links, and pinky ring. As Joe crossed to a chair, the super signed his name with a flourish on one document after another. After each signature, he flipped the executed document onto its belly, stacking one on top of the other. After he signed the last one, he picked up the pages and tamped them neatly into a meticulously squared stack, which he placed in the outbox at the corner of his desk. Looking self-satisfied, he leaned forward onto his elbows, folded his hands together, and fixed a magnanimous smile on his face.

"Joe, what can I do for you this morning? You have those reports for me already?"

"No, Vin. Actually, this is a more delicate matter," said Joe, groaning inwardly at the response he expected. He cleared his throat. "I got a phone call from Will Van Dalen's attorney. He asked whether we could allow Will to return to school immediately and get back to the basketball team."

"What?" screamed Vin as his right arm flew up simultaneously, flinging his newest Montblanc Meisterstuck 149 piston fountain pen straight up. It stuck in a panel of the drop ceiling alongside the others. "You have to be fucking kidding me!" His face flamed a bright, ruddy red, spittle flying from his fast-moving lips. His collar grew tight around his neck, and his veins and arteries bulged outward like those of an enraged bull.

"I'm sick and tired of fucking lawyers sticking their big fat noses into my business! We run this school as we see fit and that's our responsibility!" he screamed. "Who the fuck do those people think they are? I'm the super here! It's my school and I'll make these decisions and Goddamn them to hell if they want to try and change it!"

Here, Vin had to stop to get a couple of gasping breaths, his eyes still bulging, his mouth hanging open as if he had just run a 200-meter sprint. Joe wouldn't have been surprised to see him suddenly clutch his chest and keel over, dead from cardiac arrest.

"So go tell this attorney to fuck off!" More gasps. "Who is it, anyway? Who'd they hire?"

"It's Declan Fennelly."

"Oh, Declan!" A huge smile crossed the super's face as he fell back against his plump chair. "Declan's one of the good guys." He swiveled back and forth in his chair. "So what does Declan really want?"

"He wants me to talk to you and see whether Will can get back to the basketball team right away. Will's captain of the team."

"Yeah, yeah," said Vin, waving off the issue. "Whadda you think the Board of Ed will say if we bring Will back just like that and put him back out in public as captain of the basketball team?"

"I'm concerned that they may feel we've made this decision without consulting them. And while these decisions are really within the discretion of the school administration—you and me, of course—the board members may feel slighted if we terminate Will's discipline given the nature of Will's alleged crime and public sentiment." What Joe was really thinking was that the Board of Ed might be angry enough not to renew Joe's and Vin's contracts next year.

The super gazed into the corner of his office for a moment. Turning to Joe, he said, "Why don't you call the board president and run Declan's request by him first? If you get a positive response, then you can attend the closed session the board's having on

Monday night and take a poll. That way, you can build some support—if there is any—and you can give Declan what he wants without getting our asses in hot water."

My ass, you mean, thought Joe. Vin Flowers was known for distancing himself from the politically difficult issues if he could help it. That way, he kept the Board of Ed happy and continued to get favorable contracts for himself.

Joe knew he had to play his cards wisely in presenting this issue to the board president. He couldn't look as if he was in favor of bringing Will back before he'd served his full disciplinary sentence or the board would see that as traitorous. After all, they'd given him plenty of shit when he stuck up for Will after the news of Will's arrest spread through the school like a common cold in an overheated office.

No, thought Joe. I'll have to blame it on Declan and a threatened lawsuit or something. And if it doesn't work, it doesn't work. At least I'll have done what Declan asked, and that should keep me out of trouble.

A mere 35 minutes later, Joe had made his request via telephone and had been quickly set straight on how uninterested the board president was in letting Will off the hook. The reality was, he told Joe, it wasn't that he necessarily thought Will was a bad kid or had been the villain in the Ryan Sullivan matter, but that he didn't want the school district to take the heat publicly over what influential citizens and district parents saw as inappropriate leniency in a case that had drawn state-wide scrutiny.

"No siree," the board president had said. "We aren't going to get the wrong kind of reputation in this town. It could sully our upscale family atmosphere in Ocean Beach."

"So, not on my watch," he'd said. "Go back and tell Declan Fennelly that we aren't changing Will Van Dalen's disciplinary consequences, and that he and the Van Dalens had better not push it because the board members are considering expelling Will from school."

Joe put his proverbial tail between his legs and called Declan's office. He was pleased to hear that Declan was with a client. Arlene connected him with Declan's voice mail, and Joe waited patiently through the polished message advising him to leave his name, phone number, and a brief message, and Declan would return the call at his earliest convenience.

I hope not, thought Joe. I've had about enough of this.

"Declan," he said after the beep. "It's Joe Andersen. I've met with our superintendent and have spoken with the board president. It's not good news.

Not only will they not consider shortening Will's suspension, they're considering expelling him as well. If you push this issue, I think the board may move in that direction. I'm sorry, Declan. I like Will. He's a nice kid. I hope everything works out for him."

Declan listened to the message twice. The click! at the end sounded like the end of Will's dreams of a college education.

Shit, thought Declan. Now what? I could appeal the decision, but a lot of good that will do.

Appeals first had to be taken to the Ocean Beach Board of Education, the same body that was telling him that he'd better back off or they'd expel this kid. And, sure, he could even appeal the board's ruling if—no, when, he thought—it ruled against Will, but that would go up to the state commissioner of education.

Declan wasn't born yesterday. In fact, he was feeling every one of his 63 years. He believed that this hierarchy would rule in the school district's favor every time. Additionally, he was not experienced in that legal arena.

For Declan, this was a clear-cut criminal matter that should never have begun in the first place. He knew that he could bring other factors into his role as advisor to the Van Dalens, such as Will's education and his discipline by school officials, but he didn't see that as his central role. He believed himself competent as an advisor. Indeed, he never even questioned it. Now that he was aware of the school's decision, it was his duty to communicate that to his client and to get Will into PTI as soon as possible. Then this mess would simply go away. Or so he hoped.

Chapter Thirty-Three

B ill had finished his turkey sub and was starting to feel more human. He was just about to head back to the office for what he hoped would be a productive afternoon when his cell phone rang. Pulling it out of his pocket, he saw Declan's number on the digital readout.

"Declan," he said eagerly. "Have you heard anything?" He almost despised himself for his pathetic urgency.

"Bill," said Declan. "I'm glad I reached you." *Well, there's a lie,* thought Declan. "I'm afraid I've got some bad news for you."

Bill felt himself go cold all over. His hand clenched the phone more tightly. All he could say was, "Tell me."

After Declan relayed the bad news, Bill asked, "Can they do that? I live in town! I pay taxes, for Christ's sake! How can they do that?"

"Bill, I think the best thing to do is to try and get PTI as soon as we can, let Will finish his suspension, and not rock the boat by pushing for him to return sooner. If we do that, we may be fighting an expulsion instead."

"But that's blackmail!" said Bill.

"I know it feels like it, Bill, but school districts have broad discretion in these matters, and I don't want to take steps that harm your—or Will's—interests."

Bill put his face in his hand even as he clutched his cell phone to his ear. "Jesus Christ," he said. "Can't we catch a break here?"

Chapter Thirty-Four

Will sat at his desk, struggling with a writing assignment. He kept rereading the passage in front of him, but it just didn't seem to make sense. He wished he were in English class with Miss Cameron, who answered all of his questions and spent extra time with him, helping him break down the assignments and giving him prompts to help him start the writing process. His IEP said that teachers *had* to do that, but Miss Cameron did it because she was a good teacher. She liked to teach and she liked Will. He could tell. She gave him good ideas that were easy to understand, and she was nice about it. Some of his other teachers only did the barebones modifications his IEP called for—if he was lucky— but he knew sometimes they thought he was just being lazy and were exasperated with him. At those times, he felt kind of ashamed and couldn't bring himself to stay after class and ask questions; it was just too belittling. So, he put on a show of bravado here and there. He'd learned all about that from playing sports, and he was good at it. His natural athleticism lent him an easy grace in his physical self, and that at least gave him a measure of self-confidence. On the field, the court, and in the gym, Will was a leader.

Will realized he was daydreaming about Miss Cameron leaning down next to him and speaking to him in her clear and gentle voice. He could almost smell her shampoo, her female scent, which he found comforting. A sudden stab of pain through his belly made him realize he was missing his mother, missing the constant love and affection with which she had showered him. Though he loved his dad, his mother had been the more constant presence, making him dinner, doing his laundry, listening to the stories of his day, hugging him, and touching him as mothers do.

His sadness surged and pushed him to his feet. He was restless, turning here and there in his room. Feeling claustrophobic, he headed downstairs, only to be met in the kitchen by his father coming in through the garage.

"Dad." He blinked a couple of times. "You're home early."

Bill struggled for evenness in his voice, but he was too pent up to speak gently. "We need to talk," he said, unable to meet Will's eyes.

"Okay."

Bill headed into the living room and found his

La-Z-Boy by habit. Will sat on the couch, leaning forward with an expectant air.

"Will, I've had a call from Declan Fennelly."

"The school officials have informed Mr. Fennelly that they're refusing to shorten your suspension."

Will leaned farther forward, elbows on knees, every muscle in his body as taut as a tightrope. "Dad, there must be something Mr. Fennelly can do. He said he'd take care of it. Can't Mr. Anderson do something? I know Mr. Anderson likes me."

"Will, I'm afraid that Mr. Anderson is the one who delivered the news to Mr. Fennelly."

"But isn't there something we can do? I've heard other students talking about appealing their grades and stuff. Sometimes it works. Can't we do something like that?"

Will's liquid brown eyes met Bill's, pleading for help and understanding, a supplication which aroused oddly-mixed feelings of pity and anger in Bill. He himself felt helpless and angry. It was all too unreal, and Bill stared back into Will's gaze, unable to move.

"Dad," said Will, asking more than declaring, "there's got to be something else we can do."

"If we try to fight the length of your suspension, the Board of Ed might expel you."

"Expel me?" Will gaped at his father. "Expel me? But how can they do that?" Here, his voice rose an octave. "I'm still the same Will Van Dalen!" Will leaped to his feet. "I haven't changed. I'm the same person I was last week. Joking around with the guys at practice, waving 'hi' to Mr. Anderson in the hall. He smiled at me. Why is everyone suddenly treating me so differently? I didn't *do* anything."

Will didn't want to think anymore. He wanted to get away from this conversation, this room, this town where people had only pretended to like him.

"Where are you going?" Bill asked.

"I don't know. I just have to go."

"It's a school night, Will. And I don't want you going out like this after everything that's happened."

"Ha! A school night." He whirled to face Bill. "What difference does that make? It's not a school night for me. And after getting arrested for something I didn't do, and getting attacked in the park in my own neighborhood, what else could happen?" He turned toward the door.

"Will, it *is* a school night. You still have work to do, and you have to stay in shape so that when this is over in a few weeks you can go right back to playing ball. You need to stay fit, mentally and physically."

"Dad, they're not gonna let me play ball again.

It's no good anymore. I've been suspended. I'm facing trial, maybe jail time." Will sat at the bottom of the stairs and began stuffing his feet into his sneakers. "People talk about me wherever I go. Even my friends have to contact me on the sly."

"Will, don't think like that. It's defeatist. That's not like you. We'll get through this."

"Will we, Dad? I'm not so sure."

Will opened the front door and stepped out into the cold night, slamming the door shut behind him.

Wait, Will, Bill called silently. *Isn't tonight your counseling appointment?*

But Will had forgotten.

Chapter Thirty-Five

The streetlights flashed by as Will drove, barely seeing the familiar landmarks on his street, his face colorless in the light of the dashboard. He cruised to the high school, looking at the cars in the parking lot and the lights flooding out of the high windows. He saw his friends' cars in a cluster by the gym door and knew they were at practice.

Suddenly, he wanted to hide so none of them would wander outside and see him looking in, like an animal barred from civilized quarters. He headed toward the cemetery where his mother and brother were buried but detoured to his counselor's office on Raymond Avenue.

His phone buzzed in his pocket. It was his dad, asking him if he had an appointment with Judy.

Oh, shit, he thought. *Did I?*

He pulled into the driveway, which Judy shared with the other tenants of the commercial property.

Nosing into an empty parking space, he pocketed his keys, and crossed the lot. It was beyond the time of his usual appointment, but he really needed some help. Judy was always saying that he could call her anytime.

When he reached her door, however, he found it locked. Peering through the window set in the door, he saw that all the lights were off.

Will leaned against the door for a second and huffed a breath into the chill air. For an instant, he could see his breath, until it disappeared.

Will walked slowly back to his car, head down, hands in his pockets, his gaze following his feet, sheathed in their red Keds, which made no sound on the black asphalt. He unlocked the Optima's door and plunked down in the driver's seat but didn't start the engine. He had nowhere to go.

He didn't want to go into any local stores because people would stare at him and gossip about him in low voices. He was the Kidnapper.

Almost like being a pedophile, he thought. *Jesus. Don't really want to go to the park, either.*

His memories of Tuesday evening were jumbled, but they had started to intrude more and more into his conscious thoughts.

What the hell was that all about? he thought. *One*

minute, I'm shooting hoops. Next thing I know, some guy wants to have a game. Okay, weird, but it would've been good to get in some practice anyway.

He had been missing his usual routine, the way the ball felt in his palm, the way it sprang back reliably, time after time, the way he could lift off the balls of his feet, and sink the ball from any position on the court.

So, okay, he fell for it. *But, holy shit, stitches from a blow to the head?*

In the back of his mind, Will knew what this was about. *What else could it be? Damn that Troy,* he thought. *My friends were right about Troy.* But even as he thought it, Will felt something more. He'd had a soft spot for Troy ever since they met in the hospital. Troy's home life sucked. He had no mother, and his father wasn't around much. Will knew that Carl Braithwaite drank too much and stayed home too little. *So it wasn't all Troy's fault,* Will thought. *He had just lost his way. And even little brothers can sometimes be a pain in the ass.*

The trouble was that Will wasn't sure what to do about Troy. Thinking about it made his head hurt. Will fired up the Optima, hung a left on Ocean Drive, and drove all the way to the inlet. He pulled into the parking lot and eased into a spot that looked out over the dark chop of the Mantopan River. The tide was headed out, out, out, mesmerizing Will with its instability and hidden depths, fleeing toward the seemingly bottomless Atlantic Ocean.

Staring out at the cold, black water, Will felt restless and alone. He thought about taking a stroll along the boardwalk but didn't want to risk meeting anyone he knew. Instead, he reversed the Optima and drove across town to Route 209 North, and crossed the bridge over the river.

He needed to be away, somewhere he could be anonymous. When he saw the Mantopan sign, with an arrow pointing at the second exit, he impulsively hung a right. He cruised up Route 120 until he reached Main Street in Mantopan where he turned right toward the beach. On the left, just before the train tracks, was a 7-Eleven, its bright lights inviting on a cold, windy night.

Will turned into the parking lot. He went inside just for something to do and to mix with human beings, even if they were strangers. He thought about getting a Slurpee but asked for a pack of Marlboros and a lighter. *Hell*, he thought, *if I'm not gonna play ball, I don't have to worry about my wind.* The thought of harming himself gave him an edgy, high feeling.

Will stepped out of the 7-Eleven in this altered state and walked to the end of the building. He peeled off the cellophane and tamped the pack of cigarettes in his left palm, all the while looking diagonally across the street at the train tracks, the red-and-white striped crossing gate, and the train station just beyond. He pulled out a smoke and lit it, inhaling deep into his lungs, then coughed uncontrollably. He thought of stories he'd heard about kids who deliberately cut their arms and legs to distract themselves from emotional pain.

Self-mutilating, thought Will. *That's what I'm doing now, but from the inside out.*

He took another drag of his cigarette. He hadn't smoked since his mother had died. During her hospitalization, Will had blown through a pack every couple of days just to calm his nerves. Now Will wanted to laugh, but it wasn't funny. So he just stood and stared and smoked, the wind whipping around his head. It lifted his hair up and caressed him, like the invisible arms of the night, wooing him and drawing him out. He felt comforted somehow, the nicotine already pumping through his blood, giving him a sense of power and well-being.

As Will stared into the darkness, the red lights on the crossing gates started to flash and the bells clanged rhythmically. He watched the gates lower and block the roadway. He heard the train on the northbound side of the tracks give its approaching whistle. A moment later, the train pulled into the station, its single headlight like a Cyclops cutting through the darkness. He could smell the asbestos from the brakes as the train screeched to a stop only 25 yards away.

As Will stared, hardly aware of the passengers disembarking, he suddenly remembered the student who had jumped to his death in front of this train only a day earlier. He thought: *He had more to live for than I do.*

The asbestos haze thickened as he watched, swirling and mystical. The crowd of passengers hurried past him in the other direction. The clanging grew louder as he approached, the red lights pulsing in time with the beat of Will's heart. He could feel the vibrations of the train engine surging through him, soothing him.

Thoughts, potent with the unfamiliar boost of the nicotine, swirled around in his head: listening to Declan Fennelly talk about his grades and feeling shame wash over him; having his father see him in a jail cell; being attacked by an unknown assailant; the humiliation he felt when the man confronted him and his father in Joey's; learning that he was now barred from playing basketball for three weeks, which pretty much trashed his hopes of attending college.

The anonymous conductor called, "All Aboard!"

Will stared at the huge locomotive as it slowly inched forward, picking up speed as it came toward him. He imagined what it would feel like to slide into oblivion under the enormous engine and felt a surge of excitement at the thought of doing something, anything, to end his pain and humiliation, to spare his father the public embarrassment of having a son tried in the court system like a common criminal, the huge legal expenses. His head buzzed and the buzzing increased as he approached the engine.

He could accomplish in a single act what his father and Declan Fennelly had been unable to do: solve the problem. He could smell the freedom that he could give to himself, to his father. He tried to ignore the reality that his death would be the death of his father's only remaining child, indeed, his only remaining family member. He tried to rationalize this knowledge against his own urge to escape.

Maybe Dad could even get married again, thought Will, *and have more kids.*

In that moment, Will thought that his death would remove a burden from his father's shoulders. He wasn't thinking clearly or reasonably. He was acting on impulse under the influence of his mood, his thoughts, and the nicotine. *Now! Now!* shrieked the voice inside his head, and Will pictured himself moving forward.

But it was too late. As Will watched, the locomotive swept past him, and he fell back, disgusted with himself, frustrated that he hadn't followed through. He stood in the darkness as the gates lifted, his breath heaving in a sob. He turned back to the Optima.

Gunning the car out of the parking lot, Will drove

fast and thoughtlessly, seeking relief.

I'm even more of a failure now, he thought. *I can't even kill myself. I can't do anything right. I'm such a loser.* He pounded the steering wheel in frustration.

Filled with self-loathing, his anger building, Will raced toward a railroad crossing in Ocean Beach.

It's better this way, he thought. *Some kind of poetic justice to die there, where my mother and my brother died.*

His heart pounded and perspiration flowed out of the pores all over his head, crawling like worms through his hair. Desperately seeking release, Will pressed on through the night.

Coming upon the railroad crossing he was looking for, Will parked his car along the side of the road. Rolling down the windows so he could listen for the train, he turned off the lights and the ignition.

God, he thought. *If you're up there, I'll see you soon. Don't blame my dad. He did everything right. It's not his fault. He'll get over this. I'm just causing problems for him at this point. It'll be easier for him. He can make a new life.* A moment later, in quiet despair, he thought, *I know I'm a loser, but please don't turn away from me now.*

Will lit another cigarette and sat smoking quietly,

frozen in apprehension. It didn't take long before he heard the whistle of a southbound train approaching.

Will braced himself. He thought of his mother, his little brother, his friends, and the exhilaration he'd felt at his basketball games, the thunder of the crowd, the thrill of the victories. *No more,* he thought. *Never again.* He pulled open the door handle and stepped into the night.

The locomotive hurtled through the darkness at 70 miles per hour, wheels clattering, breath huffing, intent on its destination. The thrum and thunder of the engine reached a crescendo as a young man shot through the darkness toward the 200-ton cyclops. The roar rose, louder and louder, until a shriek pierced the night, the sound of screeching metal joining with human voice so seamlessly that a listener couldn't distinguish where one ended and the other began.

Chapter Thirty-Six

*S*hrieking shrieking desperate shrieking tumbling over and over and the pain the pain the pain in the red-blood haze metal and asbestos sickening smell and the pain the pain the pain was too much too much too much to bear and

Will sat straight up, screaming, covered in sweat, heart pounding, fists clutching the soaked sheet as he braced for the impact that never came.

The door flew open and his father catapulted him across the dark bedroom. "Will! Will! You're all right!" He wrapped him in a bear hug and rocked him back and forth, heart pounding against heart.

"Dad?" Will's chest heaved, the horror of his dream still clashing wildly around in his head. He could still smell the asbestos, still feel his lungs on fire with the acrid smoke and his own shrieking as he ran toward the train.

"Dad, where am I? What happened? How did I get here?"

"You're home, Will, you're home. It's the middle of the night. You're having a nightmare, that's all."

Bill's words began to seep through Will's dream state and bring him into the present.

"Oh my God, Dad, it was awful." Will paused before he could bring himself to say it out loud. "I dreamed that instead of just taking a drive last night I went to the railroad tracks and jumped in front of the train."

Bill squeezed his eyes shut more tightly.

"At the last minute, I realized I didn't really want to die, but it was too late." Will stared over his father's shoulder, thinking about the hopeless souls who had died under the North Jersey Coast Line train. Maybe, at the last minute, they hadn't really wanted to die, either.

"It's no wonder you had that dream after the week you've had." Bill took a deep, hopeful breath. "But never mind. I think I may have found a way to get you back in school. I didn't tell you tonight because I was afraid it would turn out to be nothing. I spoke with an employee of mine today who used a special-education lawyer with his school district. I think she might be able to help us. I'll call her later and make an appointment."

Will wanted to feel encouraged, but instead he felt empty and emotionally wrung out. Nonetheless, he rallied for his father's sake. "Okay, Dad, if you think so."

Chapter Thirty-Seven

When morning arrived, Bill roused Will from a deep sleep. He wanted him to come down and have breakfast with him.

As father and son sat down together in the kitchen, Bill picked up his cup, sipped his coffee, and set it back down on the table.

"Will, I'm a little concerned about you after that dream last night. Are you gonna be okay when I'm at work today?"

Will, embarrassed in the morning light by his nightmare, ducked his head. "Sure, Dad, of course."

Sensing what Will was feeling, Bill said, "Will, you don't need to be embarrassed with me. Grown men have nightmares after they've been locked up in jail. They just don't tell anybody about it. But you and I have learned some lessons from counseling, right? I myself had to use HALT yesterday, and I hope you'll use the tools Judy's given you when you need to."

Despite the difficulty of saying the words, Bill forced himself to go on. "I told you I plan to call that lawyer today. In the meantime, will you promise me that you'll be safe? And that if you think about… hurting yourself… you'll call me or Judy?"

"Dad, I promise. But even in the dream, I knew I didn't really want to die. I just wanted to find a solution to my problems."

"Suicide is a permanent solution to a temporary problem, remember? I think that you and I can do better than that."

Bill pushed back his chair, got to his feet, and took his plate over to the trash to wipe it clean. Then he stowed it in the dishwasher. "I've got to head out now. I'd like you to stick to a schedule today. Use the timer on your phone if you need to, but I want you to keep up with your schoolwork, and I want you to get some exercise, too. Okay?"

"Sounds good." Will got to his feet and gave his dad a hearty pat-on-the-back hug that communicated respect and deep love.

Feeling somewhat reassured, Bill grabbed his keys and lunch and headed out the door.

Bill arrived in his office at about ten to eight. He closed his door and got out the number for the special education attorney. Bill knew the office was probably closed, but he dialed the number and waited while the phone rang. As expected, the phone was answered by an electronic voice message: *you have reached Myler Law Group. For Elizabeth Myler, dial extension 101.* Bill pushed 1-0-1 and heard the phone ring again. Mentally rehearsing what he would say, he was startled when the phone was answered after the first ring with a crisp, "Liz Myler."

"Oh, hello, Ms. Myler. I didn't expect to reach you so early."

"With whom am I speaking?"

"My name's Bill Van Dalen. I'm calling about my son, Will Van Dalen. He's a student at Ocean Beach High School."

"Is Will a classified student?"

"He's classified as ADHD."

"Actually, ADHD is a diagnosis, not a classification. Does he have an IEP?"

"Oh. Yes, he does."

"Okay, and how old is he?"

"He's 18 years old."

"So he's an adult. Will he consent to having you involved in his educational decision-making?"

"I'm certain that he will."

"Okay. What is it that makes you call an attorney at this hour, Bill?"

Bill launched right into the story. Everything started coming out—the arrest. Overnight incarceration. The attack. How Will was really a good kid. His mother's and brother's death. The suspension. The jeopardized scholarship.

"Mr. Van Dalen, let me interrupt you. I think you need to come in for a consultation as soon as possible. The school district should have held a manifestation determination meeting for such a long suspension. It sounds as if they're in violation of the law. I'll want you to bring all of your pertinent paperwork, such as Will's latest evaluations, his IEP, any disciplinary reports— including the suspension notice. I want to hear the rest of the story, and then I'll explain how the law works, give you an analysis of your case, and tell you what your options are."

"That sounds great," said Bill. "One thing, though... money's a little tight right now..."

"I'll waive the cost of the consultation, Bill, how's that? Then we'll get you in here and see what's going on."

They scheduled a consultation for the following Tuesday morning. After Bill hung up, he felt more light-hearted than he had all week. He called Will to let him know that he had an appointment, and that, if he retained the attorney, she'd want to see Will as well.

Chapter Thirty-Eight

Friday was normally a day of optimism. The work week was about to end. Maybe it was also pizza night or date night or just chill-at-home night. But after his call with Liz Myler, Bill plunged himself back into the mountain of paperwork on his desk. Business was still slow and, after the drama of the week, it was simply exhaustion and gloom that accompanied Bill home from work later that day. To make things even emptier, it was after dark when he drove up to the house.

The porch light wasn't on. Bill's "I'm home!" echoed through an empty house. Bill's stomach started to churn. He'd been worried last night after Will had awoken from a nightmare and admitted he'd dreamt about killing himself. His unease returned.

"Will?" he called. Silence ensued.

Bill checked the garage. No Optima. *Where the heck is Will?* He was irritated.

Just then, the front door banged open.

"Hey, Dad!"

Bill met his son in the front hallway. "Where were you?"

"Just riding around," said Will, hanging up his letter jacket in the front closet. "I thought I'd get out of the house for a while." He sat down on the bottom step of the staircase to remove his sneakers.

"Okay, next time, let me know where you're going," said Bill, feeling like a puckered-up old worrywart. The starch suddenly went out of him, and he leaned against the doorframe.

Will stood up and Bill realized that his son was now taller than he.

"Dad, are you okay?"

"Not really. Let's go sit down for a minute."

Frowning, Will followed his dad into the living room.

When they were seated next to the fireplace, Bill began, "I know I may have seemed tense lately…"

Will put his hands up. "Dad, it's okay. I'm sorry. It's my fault. I'm sorry about all of the trouble I've caused you."

Bill shook his head. "No, no, Will. That's not it.

Or *just* it. I'm having some issues at work. I didn't want you to think that it's your fault."

"What kind of issues, Dad?"

Bill heaved a sigh, sat back in his chair, and closed his eyes for a moment.

"I haven't been myself for a long time, not since your mother and Patrick…"

Will leaned forward. "Dad…"

"It's about time I said it. I just couldn't get it together, and it's been affecting business. It's been so hard to keep my mind focused at work. Truth is, I haven't been that organized. I've mixed up orders. I haven't always called customers back…"

"I'm sure people understand, Dad, don't you think?"

"For a while, they did, Will, but that only goes so far. I run a business, not a charity. People pay for services and products, and they don't want to hear excuses."

"Anyway, I've been having a little trouble keeping up with the bills. A while back, I found out that one of my major accounts is terminating our contract."

"What does that mean, Dad?"

"It means we're on the edge of bankruptcy."

Chapter Thirty-Nine

Unfortunately, Bill's little fireside chat with his son had the opposite of its intended effect. As Will tried to sleep that night, he kept seeing his father looking as if the life had gone out of him. All he could think was *If only. If only I hadn't pressed Mom to pick me up after practice that night. If only I hadn't blindly followed Troy. If only I hadn't gone out that night. If only I'd been smarter about it. If only, if only.*

The more he thought about it, the more he thought things had gone to shit.

I'm such a fuck up. Dad's been carrying this load around, trying to deal with everything, and then I act like such a kid. Getting fucking arrested. Getting suspended. Losing my chance to go to college. I can't make the grade—literally can't make the grade, so no chance for any academic scholarship there. And now Dad's got all these legal bills on top of everything else. I have to do something. I can't just leave him to deal with this mess on his own.

Then he realized: *Duh. I'll get a job. I'm not in school right now. I can't play basketball, so Dad can't object if I get a job. At least I can do that much.*

Chapter Forty

Waves crashed onto the sand as Will gazed off into the distance. The sky was a gray mirror of his mood. After a restless night, he'd gotten up and out of the house early, determined to land a job. He'd shaved, put on a button-down shirt, and brushed his hair.

Feeling optimistic and energized, he'd been to every business in and out of town that might offer him a position: Home Depot, Lowe's, UPS, FedEx, ShopRite, Trader Joe's, Whole Foods, even the local pet shop and a diner. It had been the same result at each place: Once they realized who he was, they politely told him they had no positions available—every place, that is, except the pet shop, where the owner had given him a piece of his mind about young men who sold drugs. Threatening to get his shot gun and blow Will "into next week," he'd run him out of the store so fast Will had almost fallen onto the sidewalk.

Will had ended up at the beach, staring into the

water. Feeling morose and tired, he drifted off… only to be awakened by a pounding on the window. Jerking awake, Will saw a police officer peering into the window.

"Hey, Van Dalen!" he roared. "This ain't your boudoir. You wanna nap, go home." Punctuating his order with a glare, the officer stalked off.

Shaken, feeling buzzy with no sleep and a lack-of-sleep hangover, he headed toward home.

Maybe that's where I belong right now, anyway, he thought. *No one wants anything to do with me. The school, the team. Coach. The cops, the stores. Probably even Dad.* Not since his mother's and brother's deaths had Will felt so alone. His chest constricted. Nothing felt normal anymore.

Chapter Forty-One

Troy blinked his crusty eyes open sometime on Saturday afternoon but closed them again. Thoughts he wanted to avoid swirled in his mind. Will laughing. Will pulling up in the Optima to take him to a game. Out for pizza. To the park to shoot some hoops. *Christ, Will is more like family to me than my own brother,* he thought. *More than my own parents. And I ratted him out.*

With a groan, he rolled over onto his belly and buried his face in the pillow, but the pictures kept intruding: the interview with the cops when he fingered Will. Will on the front porch, his anger lit like a fuse on a stick of dynamite after Troy taunted him. Ratting him out to Guzman.

Shame and self-loathing welled up inside him. He curled up into a ball and clenched his eyes more tightly, fighting for peace. Or, at least, oblivion.

Chapter Forty-Two

On Saturday evening, fortified with a couple of tacos and a coke from Surf Taco, Will rode a new crest of hope and determination to the job hunt. He drove about half an hour to two popular restaurants that catered to the well-heeled and to a couple of big-box stores.

At first, no one recognized Will at any of these locations, and he was given a job application to fill out. But when he got to the part which asked about his criminal history, Will was stymied. He didn't want to lie. On the other hand, he didn't want to tell the truth.

If I write that I've been arrested, I'll have to say why, he thought as he stood at the counter, chewing his lip and shifting back and forth from left foot to right. *Then for sure, they won't hire me. But if I don't put it down and they find out, I'll lose the job anyway.*

He glanced up at the woman behind the service counter. Just at that second, she looked up and caught his gaze. She removed her reading glasses and came over.

"All done?" she asked, holding out her hand.

"Uh, no." He gave her a crooked little smile. "I'm gonna take this with me." He waved the application form around. "I'll bring it back when I'm finished."

The woman gave him a strange look, shrugged her shoulders, and said, "Okay, sure."

Will slunk away, application in hand.

Chapter Forty-Three

M usic was blaring over speakers later on Saturday night as Troy entered the crush of teenage bodies in the finished basement. Technically, he hadn't been invited to this party; he'd heard about it from a kid he'd sold a couple of joints to.

Whatever, he thought. *No one will notice. They're all either drunk or stoned out of their minds. Someone could've invited me. Hey, I invited myself.*

He chuckled, but it was an effort. He'd really come because he couldn't stand the thoughts running around in his head like squirrels on a wheel, couldn't even stand himself. The more noise and distraction, the better, and here he was, in the midst of the din.

Troy headed toward the other side of the room where he saw a keg on a table. He'd heard through the grapevine that Kevin Donoghue's parents were out of town for the weekend, and Kevin was all party hearty. There were so many kids in the room that Troy had to push his way through the bodies, all warm, undulating, and excited on this Saturday night.

The upbeat mood was infectious, and Troy found himself caught up in its buoyancy. The three Solo cups of beer he'd sucked down hadn't hurt, either. Now he found himself engaged in conversation with Tina Martelli, a pixy-ish blond sophomore whose eyes sparkled when she talked. He was so relaxed he didn't feel the need for a smoke until she excused herself to go to the "little girls' room." Troy took the opportunity to head out back for a quick cigarette since the "party hearty" theme didn't extend to smoking cigarettes in the house.

Troy's lighter flicked as eyes, watching in the night, saw the flame flash and light up Troy's face. The cigarette glowed as Troy inhaled deeply and felt the first moment's peace he'd had in days.

It didn't last. Out of the darkness emerged six or eight—it was hard to tell exactly; it was so dark and it happened so fast—older, larger boys who surrounded Troy. His stomach sank. He was aware of a sudden panic and the odd thought *déjà vu all over again* before he was shoved from behind.

He staggered forward, arms reflexively flailing to steady himself, and bumped into the beefy guy in front of him.

"Hey, watch where you're going!" The guy

pushed Troy back.

Arms caught him from behind, strong arms painfully grasping his upper arms.

"Oh, hey, it's Troy. Troy Braithwaite."

Another shove to the other side of the small circle of friends.

"Troy Braithwaite? You mean Will's friend?"

Those arms thrust him sideways, knocking him off balance and into a tall, musclebound jock.

"Troy is no friend of Will Van Dalen's. He's the druggie who got Will in trouble."

"You little shit! Why don't you just disappear, huh? The world would be better off without you. Why don't you just crawl in a hole and die?"

"No idea what Will sees in you. You're more trouble than you're worth. Way more."

"Yeah, he's a little shit. No wonder his mother left."

The pushing became swift and violent. All the while the boys called, "You little shit. Who do you think you are? We warned Will about you. We should kick the shit out of you."

Troy was lost in the chaos of this violent tirade. His head was spinning. He tried to grab onto the boys so he wouldn't fall, but they shoved him back and forth so fast, he couldn't get a grip. He could feel himself heating up.

Suddenly, the sour brew in his stomach spewed out of his mouth like a geyser.

"Jesus Christ!"

They shoved him to the ground, trying to shake Troy's puke off of themselves and kicking dirt on him.

"You're disgusting, man."

"Let's get outta here," one of them said.

Pairs of feet thudded off, amidst cursing. A silence ensued, but Troy didn't notice it. He was a sobbing mess, curled in on himself physically and mentally. Time ticked by, but Troy paid no attention to how long he lay there, alone, gravel digging into his cheek, snot running out of his nose. He was oblivious to physical discomfort; all the injury was in his mind, where the damage of the past swirled up to meet the night's new darkness. The result was a storm raging through his psyche, a torrent unleashed like a ferocious, rampaging beast, tearing at his thoughts, his tenuous connection to sanity.

You're more trouble than you're worth, Troy. His mother's words pounded through his head like a drumbeat that he could feel, as well as hear.

You little shit! Why don't you just disappear, huh? The world would be better off without you. Why don't you just crawl in a hole and die? You're more trouble than you're worth, Troy.

Chapter Forty-Four

Somehow, Troy made it home from the party. He didn't remember how. He didn't want to remember the previous night. In fact, there was a whole lot of his life he was desperately trying to erase. That's why he slept until the afternoon.

He'd woken earlier to someone moving around in the kitchen. *Must be Marc,* he thought. *He's the only one who's really human in this house. Probably going off to work. Time to make the doughnuts.* He pulled the covers up over his head.

It was a gray day anyway, and that made it easier for Troy to put off the inevitable for as long as possible. But ultimately, the human bladder can hold only so much, and even young bones ache when lying for too long. Late in the afternoon, Troy sat up, feet on the floor, head in his hands.

Late to the party again, eh, Troy boy? he mocked himself. *That doesn't really matter since no one wants you there anyway. Everyone says you're more trouble than you're worth. Everyone knows it. Your mother knew it for sure. That's why she booked it outta here a long time ago. Nothing to hold her here. Nothing to tempt the milk of motherly kindness in this joint. Not even her baby.*

Troy tried to clamp down on the negative tides washing through his mind and making him miserable, making his stomach hurt.

Nah, he thought. *I just need some food. I'll go see what Dad's up to.*

After he'd emptied his bladder—filling the john with recycled beer tainted with misery—and washed up, Troy went off in search of something. Maybe coffee. He carried some hope that his dad would scramble him a couple of eggs with yellow American cheese on toast—cheesy eggs, they used to say. He'd loved that as a kid… when Mom was home, when Dad was happy and sober.

As on so many other days, Troy's meager hopes were dashed, and he knew it before he saw it— smelled it. The putrid stink of vomit preceded his entry into the TV room, where he found his father passed out on the rug, cold chunky puke all over the couch. For one horrible moment Troy thought his father was dead. He looked like a corpse, his face gray and waxy.

His father snorted, shivered, and rolled onto his

side. Troy had never been so glad to see such a disgusting sight.

It *was* disgusting, though, and it was clear that Carl Braithwaite wouldn't be cooking eggs for his son.

Troy went to the kitchen and shuffled through, brewing some coffee. He carried it into his bedroom and smoked a few cigarettes. The caffeine and nicotine coursed through his 135-pound body, momentarily rejuvenating him.

Without thinking, Troy reached for the shoebox and its maternal memorabilia. He had sorted through it day and night this week. Merely touching those items had brought him back to earlier days, when he'd felt loved and protected.

For the first time ever, though, this ritual failed to soothe Troy's troubled soul. Over and over, he replayed the events of the past week: getting pizza with Will, feeling happy. Jumping on Ryan in the back of Will's car, feeling rage. His interview with Detective Graham. His face burned with shame so that he could hardly face that memory. He'd been a coward and had thrown Will under the proverbial bus. Will didn't deserve that. On top of that, he'd fallen into the frightful huddle of the football team, and older boys nearly twice his size had shoved him around violently, like a toy punching bag—the kind that bounced back up when you smacked it to the floor, ready for another hit. He still heard their voices in his head.

The druggie who got Will in trouble.

You're more trouble than you're worth.

He's a little shit. No wonder his mother left.

The worst cut, the deepest cut, was Will pulling up after being arrested. Troy now realized that Will hadn't even been angry when he'd come to see him, but Troy had been defensive and degrading, and then Will had exploded, and every word was seared into Troy's brain:

"My friends warned me about you. They said you were trouble. I stuck up for you, you little bastard. But they were right. You're more trouble than you're worth."

Over and over, those words thundered through Troy's brain, growing louder and louder, larger and larger.

You're more trouble than you're worth, Troy. You're more trouble than you're worth.

Troy could see Will's mouth, larger than life, voicing his disgust, over and over as the words reverberated through the chambers of Troy's mind. Then the talking mouth turned into his mother's red lips and white teeth, sneering at him. That day, he had watched in fascination as she applied a fresh coat of lipstick, then dropped the case into her purse. Except it had dropped to the floor, and he had grabbed it.

"You're more trouble than you're worth, Troy."

Why did she say that? What did she ever have to do for him? Nothing. That was the answer. She never did a damned thing for him. That was the last time he ever saw her.

He fingered that lipstick case now, a tangible connection which always gave him comfort. This time, looking at the flimsy plastic case and the garish color, he felt nothing but clenching nausea. It gripped him and he felt his emotions plummet.

Wildly, he looked around the room. He felt short of breath, and needed to get away. He threw on shoes and a hoodie, and passed his father on the way out the door. Carl mumbled at him, still only partially conscious.

"I'm going to 7-Eleven."

The town was cloaked in twilight as Troy made his way to 7-Eleven, ostensibly for more coffee and cigarettes. In reality, he needed to escape the oppression—and the stench—of his house. But they pursued him; they were making him crazy. He could not rest from them. He walked on, not seeing the street, but seeing the boys pushing him back and forth, jeering at him.

He had escaped from them physically, but their hatred had only piggy-backed on his mother's hatred of him, and his own hatred of himself. He actually wished they *had* kicked the shit out of him. He deserved it. Will had done nothing but be kind to him, befriend him, even protect him. In short, Will had treated him like a real brother, as if he really cared. It had been a long time since Troy's own father or brother had extended that kind of care and concern.

Troy hung his head in shame.

Look how I repaid him, Troy thought, feeling new and ever-more-powerful feelings of self-disgust.

He was suddenly so tired of this burden.

Images of Will snarling in his face swirled with his mother's calm, cold indifference, exploding in a painful warp he knew he had to escape. His fists knuckled his eyes as he muttered to himself.

He began to run. Blindly. Toward his hoped-for oblivion. In the distance, the train whistle sounded. He ran faster.

Chapter Forty-Five

Will had spent Sunday simultaneously avoiding his father and searching online for a solution to his conflict. How should he answer the job application questions about whether he'd ever been arrested or convicted of a crime?

I haven't been convicted of a crime, he reasoned. *But I have been arrested. And for more than one crime. I've been charged with crimes. I've appeared in court in front of a judge, and right now I'm out on bail.*

It sounded so terrible, even he wouldn't hire himself.

Is that discrimination? he wondered. Nevertheless, he was sure that if he told the truth, no one would hire him. If he lied about it and the lie was discovered, he'd probably be fired on the spot. *Could they make me repay my wages?* he wondered. It was all quite confounding, and Will felt exhausted.

He needed some help to work through it, but he couldn't ask his dad.

He's got enough on his mind, Will thought. *How about Mr. Fennelly? Nah, he'd tell my dad, and then I'd be right back where I started, dumping this on my dad's head.*

Will stood up from his desk. *No, I have to figure this out on my own. But how? Who else can I talk to?* He paced. *Aunt Dana? Ppffft,* he thought, and shook his head. *I'd get an earful from her, and she'd probably tell Dad, too.* He paced some more. *Coach Lichtenberg? He probably doesn't wanna give me the time of day.* He thought of his friends, but they were all athletes. He already felt small and stupid, as if he'd let them down, especially after they'd warned him about Troy. *No,* thought Will. *I can't ask them. Who's left? Troy?*

Hell, no. But I do need to have a different kind of talk with Troy. He's gotta go back to the police station and tell the cops the truth.

Day was turning into night when Will backed out of the driveway and headed over to Troy's. Troy's father, looking pretty wasted for a Sunday and smelling even worse than he looked, informed Will that Troy wasn't home. No, Mr. Braithwaite had no idea where Troy had gone. Maybe to 7-Eleven for cigarettes.

As Will headed down Broadway toward the 7-Eleven, he heard the southbound North Jersey Coast Line train sound its whistle in the distance. Will felt a prickle up the back of his neck. It gave him an eerie feeling. Suddenly in the distance, he saw a figure running away from him.

He pressed down on the accelerator, closing the distance. Was that Troy? It *was* Troy. Why was he running toward the 7-Eleven? *Did he see me? Is he running away from me?*

Will gunned the Optima's engine and pulled off the road in a spray of gravel.

"Troy!" he called. "Troy, wait!"

But Troy didn't wait. It didn't look like Troy had even heard him. He had a wild look on his face.

The train whistle sounded again, louder this time. The clackety-clack of the wheels indicated the locomotive was still on the train bridge. Once it reached the other side, it would be only seconds before it sped past.

Will had a sudden flash of understanding. Adrenaline shot to his heart, and he shot out of his car, running after Troy.

"Troy, no! Troy! Don't do it!"

Troy's thin figure sped toward the tracks. The locomotive was beyond the bridge now. The gates on

Broadway were down, red lights blinking, bells clanging, warning that the train was about to thunder past at 70 miles per hour. And Troy was on a path to meet the train head on.

Will's legs kicked into high gear, flying through the darkness. The clackety-clack of the wheels grew louder, nightmarish. The diesel train raced through the night as it bore down on Troy's pathetic figure. Will was almost there, almost there…

Will cried out with one last great effort and leaped at the running figure.

"Troy!"

Down they crashed, Will on top, sliding and rolling together down the embankment, away from the mesmerizing wheels, the deafening engine thundering through the air, the earth, and their bodies, rumbling into the distance.

Will lay on top of Troy, lungs heaving, pinning the younger boy to the gravel. Troy, a gaunt figure with tears cutting through the soot on his face, began sobbing.

"Troy! You scared the shit outta me." Will grabbed Troy's shoulders and gave him a little shake. "What were you thinking?"

Troy knuckled the tears out of his eyes, unable to meet Will's gaze.

"I'm better off dead," he replied.

"C'mon, man, that's crazy!"

"That's not what you said the other day," said Troy. "You said I was more trouble than I'm worth. Just like my mother. That's what she used to say."

Guilt washed over Will. He felt even smaller now than when his father had bailed him out of jail. But he also felt stronger, and he felt a resolution rise within him.

"That's just bullshit, Troy. I was just mad, and, to tell you the truth, I was hurt. You lied to the police about me."

Troy said nothing and kept his gaze averted.

"But I realized something that day. Brothers do that sometimes. Sometimes we hurt each other and say stupid things. I didn't know your mom said that to you too. That's terrible."

Will sat up, sorting out his thoughts. Troy was in a fragile state, and there'd be time later for recrimination and paybacks.

Troy sat up in the gravel and faced him.

"We're friends," Will said. "Maybe more than that. After my mom and brother died, I kind of adopted you as my little brother. And that's for keeps.

Troy, unable to speak, put his hands to his mouth

and started sobbing again.

Will wrapped his big brother's arms around Troy, saying, "It's okay. It's okay. You're gonna be okay."

Will pulled away and gave Troy a pretend slap to each cheek. "C'mon, c'mon, we gotta get goin'. We can't sit around all day waiting for the train. How about if I treat you to a coffee? But no cigarettes, okay?"

Chapter Forty-Six

Troy and Will took their coffees to the inlet, where they sat and talked while the moon shone on the inky surface of the water that undulated in front of them. They shared stories of their families. Will told Troy how he missed his mother and brother and felt guilty about their deaths. Troy opened up about how his mother had abandoned the family, and the damage she'd done before leaving.

They stayed long after their coffees had grown cold.

The next morning, a Monday morning, was Halloween. Troy still felt raw and vulnerable. When he thought of Will saving his life, he was jubilant. Someone actually cared about him, enough to come after him and stop him from ending his miserable life. Maybe it wasn't so miserable after all.

By turns, however, he also felt even worse now. Will was a saint. Or, at least, a real brother. He hadn't deserved to be framed, and Troy was the one who'd done it. Troy tried slipping into the blessed blackness of sleep, but he merely tossed and turned in his bed. He didn't get up for school and, big surprise, his father didn't bother to wake him or ask him why he wasn't up and ready. Probably because Carl wasn't up and ready for work—if he still had a job.

Troy rolled onto his back and faced the ceiling. Dread weighed heavily on his chest, but he knew what he had to do.

Chapter Forty-Seven

The Halloween sun was low in the sky as Troy stepped out of the police department.

Troy loved Halloween. He still went door-to-door trick-or-treating. He didn't make much of an effort with a costume; he just wore his usual gray hoodie and jeans with some white makeup and black lipstick. He carried an old pillowcase to collect his candy.

This year, however, he barely noticed the little kids going around with their parents. Pulling a red-and-white cardboard pack out of his pocket, Troy lit a cigarette and took a deep drag. He closed his eyes as he felt the nicotine course through his system, smoothing him out.

Man, that had been rough. Worse, because it hadn't gone the way he'd expected. It had been hard enough going in there to fess up, telling the cops he had lied and that he was the one who'd sold the drugs to Ryan Sullivan and held a knife to Ryan's neck.

Yeah, that had been hard. What Troy hadn't expected, though, was that the cop didn't even believe him.

Officer Brandt had led Troy back into the same interrogation room he'd been in the first time he'd come to the station in the detective's car. A few minutes later, Detective Graham came in and heard Troy's story.

"You're saying that you lied under oath the last time you were here? That you completely made up the story about Will Van Dalen selling the drugs and threatening Ryan Sullivan with a knife?"

When Troy confirmed, the detective sat back, at war with himself. Here was this kid, whom they'd been surveilling for drug activity, telling him that Will Van Dalen, a star athlete in town, was innocent. Yet Detective Graham just knew that Van Dalen must be implicit somehow, some way. He thought he was relying on his cop sense. He was unaware that he was really biased by his own jealousy.

He fixed Troy with a stern look.

"Now, Troy, you can tell me if Mr. Van Dalen has threatened you. What has he said or done to you that made you come in today with this story?"

"I'm telling you, man, Will didn't do nothin'. He doesn't even know I'm here."

"Then why are you here?"

"Because, man, because it's not right. What I did wasn't right. I framed Will—he didn't know anything about the weed or Ryan owing me money. It was *my* weed. I sold it to Ryan and Ryan owed me money. Will didn't know that's why I wanted to swing by Ryan's."

It had taken the better part of two hours, and the officer had made Troy go through the story several times. Finally, the officer had to end the interview and have Troy sign a new statement.

But, wow. Detective Graham really thought that Will had done it. He had accepted Troy's confession very reluctantly.

I don't get it, thought Troy. *I thought that would be the easy part. I thought it would clear up the whole problem. I thought I was doing something good. But I guess they just had to make sure I was telling the truth this time,* he thought. *Especially since Will's technically an adult.*

Shaking himself, he crushed the cigarette butt under his shoe and hiked off down the sidewalk toward home.

Safely ensconced in his own room, Troy texted Will.

I have good news

Okay

Went back to the cops today

And

I told them the truth

No shit? What'd they say?

Didn't believe me at first. Finally took my statement. Spilled my guts. Now they know you didn't do it.

Will leaped up to tell his dad the good news. Bill, jubilant, wasted no time in calling Declan Fennelly. Declan promised to call the prosecutor first thing in the morning to move the ball along.

"Looks like the tide has turned." Bill beamed at his son.

Chapter Forty-Eight

On Tuesday morning, Bill found himself squirming in his chair in a waiting room lined with legal tomes along one of its walls. His stomach was clenched, and he realized how very desperate he was that this attorney would be able help to his son. He literally felt at a dead end, and he was praying that Liz Myler would lead him to the invisible door that would bring him and Will to a better place.

The internal door opened, and he looked up to see a brunette in a navy business suit. Despite his distracted state of mind, Bill was momentarily awestruck by her dark-haired beauty, her wide and welcoming smile, and her fit and shapely figure. She greeted him with a smile. "Mr. Van Dalen? I'm Liz Myler. Please come in."

Momentarily mesmerized, Bill did as she requested, following Liz to her office and taking a seat. When Liz asked to see the documents he'd brought, Bill realized he was clutching a manila folder. As he handed them over, Liz asked him for a summary of Will's school history. While Bill discussed Will's education, all of his issues came tumbling out: early signs of anxiety and discomfort with schoolwork and a diagnosis of ADHD, followed by depression and more anxiety, which exacerbated after his mother's and brother's deaths. At one point, Bill confided, Will had talked about killing himself. Bill also shared Will's dream from the previous night.

"Does Will have a plan to kill himself?"

"No, he said he really doesn't want to kill himself."

"Okay. Does Will have a significant disciplinary history in school?"

"No. In fact, he's never been suspended before this."

"The numbers indicate a high average IQ. How are his grades?"

"Last year, his grades were all 80s and 90s, but then he failed three-quarters of his final exams."

Liz glanced up at him. "Why?"

"I'm not really sure. His teachers sometimes say he's lazy. They say he's always pleasant and respectful, but he doesn't always hand work in or finish classwork."

"That might simply be a manifestation of Will's ADHD."

Liz studied the reports for another moment. "It doesn't look as if anyone has ever run a discrepancy analysis on Will to determine whether he has a specific learning disability. Some of his scores suggest that he's not achieving according to his potential, but that hasn't been explained anywhere that I can see."

"What's a specific learning disability?"

"It's when a student is not realizing his potential for an unknown reason involving the brain's ability to receive and process information. For example, Will's intelligence shows he should be achieving at a rate equivalent to his IQ, but he isn't. It may be that he learns differently than other students."

Bill sat quietly, absorbing this information.

Liz moved to Will's most recent IEP. "So I'm looking at the PLAAFP of Will's most recent IEP." She looked up at Bill. "That's the Present Levels of Academic Achievement and Functional Performance. This is where teachers and staff who work with Will report in narrative fashion how he's doing." She looked down again. "Here are some of the comments: 'Will is terribly disorganized and often loses his stuff. He recently lost his notebook. He often has trouble staying on task'... 'I know he is currently trying hard and is frustrated, but he has not come for after school help'... 'I think he is having trouble managing his time. If he is truly interested in improving, he needs to come consistently for extra help'... 'he has trouble working independently. He frequently asks questions, which I don't mind, but it is excessive.'" Liz looked up. "That's astonishing. The teacher is blaming Will for the results of his disability. Did she read his IEP? Doesn't she know that he has ADHD? These are classic symptoms. He can't keep his 'stuff' organized without some organizational assistance. He can't manage his time without being taught how to compensate for his disability. She blames him for not coming in for extra help, but then says he asks too many questions.

"And that makes me curious," said Liz as she leafed through the IEP. "Yes, that's what I thought." She looked up at Bill. "Your son's IEP has no goals and objectives to address his disabilities *whatsoever*. The IEP team should have addressed his disorganization and difficulty working independently."

Liz reviewed the rest of the IEP, then sat back, leaned her elbows on the arms of her chair, and pressed her fingertips together. "Before I start talking, Bill, let me just ask you this. What's your goal in coming here today?"

"I want Will back in school. I want him playing basketball. If he doesn't get back to school right away, he won't be seen by college coaches. He's already been told he'll likely be offered a scholarship after basketball season at one school, and some of the Division Two and Three schools are planning to come see him play. We have good reason to believe he'll get other offers, but that's only if he's playing ball."

"Okay. I think I can help you, but let me first explain how the law works and outline what I would do if you were to retain me."

"Will is classified under a federal law called IDEA. The long and short of it is that your school district must provide Will an IEP that is 'reasonably calculated' to provide him with 'significant learning' and 'meaningful educational benefit.' That benefit should be gauged according to Will's potential. That's called FAPE—a free, appropriate, public education."

Liz saw that Bill was struggling to absorb all of this. "Sorry, there's so much alphabet soup here. The good news is you don't have to remember all of this right now. Just try and get the gist." She smiled reassuringly.

"One of the most common ways to assess a student's potential is through psychological testing to obtain an IQ score. An average IQ falls between 90 and 109. A high average IQ falls between 110 and 119. Two years ago, when your district last tested Will, his IQ was in the high average range."

"Will should be achieving in the high average range, but he isn't. That's because his deficits—the symptoms of his ADHD—are adversely affecting his performance. And from what I can see in this IEP, your school district has done nothing to address Will's deficiencies in the manner required by law. There are no goals or objectives to teach Will how to manage his executive functioning deficits."

"What's that?"

"It helps to think of the planning part of the brain as an executive giving orders to the rest of the brain. You and I do this naturally. For instance, you know you need to be in the office by 8:00 a.m. Therefore, you might prepare your clothing the night before. You set your alarm for six to allow time for a shower, breakfast, making your lunch, and the drive to work."

"The brains of people with executive functioning deficiencies don't work that way. They might set the alarm for 7:30 am without having prepared their clothing. Then they get up and take a shower and realize it's eight o'clock and they're late. They rush out the door, forget their lunch, and arrive 15 minutes late looking like a train wreck."

"I'm not sure whether Will is that bad," said Bill. "But I guess I believed his teachers when they told me he was lazy."

"Will is not lazy. His teachers even say in the PLAAFP that he's hard-working. It must be incredibly frustrating for him to work so hard and then not get the grades he was hoping for. A lot of students lose their self-confidence and self-esteem under those circumstances."

"But if it's a neurological disorder," said Bill, "what can really be done about it?"

"The school district could easily assign him some time with a teacher who is specially trained to work with kids on these types of issues. That could do wonders for Will. The IEP team would just need to add some measurable goals and objectives to Will's IEP—which is in violation of the law, by the way—and the teacher could implement that instruction."

Liz continued. "Moreover, from what I can see, the district has failed to address what looks like a specific learning disability, which might require specialized instruction or a smaller class. There's no transition planning in this IEP, either, which is required once a student turns 16, years old. So, even after a perfunctory review of Will's records, I can safely say that your school district has failed its obligation to provide Will with a FAPE."

As Liz explained the law to him, Bill experienced dawning realization, disbelief, then the slow burn of anger as he realized just how significant the district's transgressions were and how much they might have affected Will.

"I can't believe this is happening," he said. "I trusted these people to do their jobs. How can they get away with this?"

"Unfortunately, this happens frequently. Parents don't know their rights. When people are unaware of their rights, they can't enforce them."

Liz continued. "There are a few more things that you need to know about what the law says, starting with IDEA, a law that provides procedural safeguards to students with disabilities. One of them is that school districts cannot discipline students for their disabilities. We have to take a look at how this whole incident with Ryan Sullivan affects Will's educational program."

"You may be aware that a Memorandum of Agreement exists in New Jersey between law enforcement and school districts."

"Yes, Will's criminal law attorney explained it to us."

"Okay, good. Then you understand that there is zero tolerance for certain kinds of behavior and that students can be disciplined for conduct that happens off school grounds."

"Actually, no, I'm not aware of that."

"Okay, then let's back up a moment. In certain situations, school authorities can discipline students for violating the school's code of conduct, even if they are off of school grounds. On the other hand, with students who have disabilities, they cannot discipline students for behavior that results from their disability.

"I know it's hard to wrap your mind around it, so let me give you an example. Say a student has Tourette Syndrome. That's a neurological disorder that causes tics, which can be exacerbated by stress. If the student starts coughing or twitching or maybe even uttering a word, the teacher can't just throw him out of class.

"For serious disciplinary issues, if a student like Will is suspended for more than 10 consecutive school days, the school district must hold the meeting I mentioned, the manifestation determination meeting."

"You mentioned that in our phone conversation. What is it, exactly?"

"That's when educators who know the student sit down with the parents to figure out whether the student's disability caused the conduct or the behavior happened because the school failed to implement the student's IEP. If the student's disability caused the behavior, then the school district must formally assess the student's behavior, must create and implement a Behavior Intervention Plan, and must return the student to the placement from which he was removed."

A smile spread across Bill's face.

"If you want me to help you return Will to school as soon as possible, here's what I'll do. First, I will immediately write a letter to your school district detailing all the deficiencies in Will's IEP and their other violations of the law. Second, I will demand an immediate manifestation determination review. Third, I will talk to Will's counselor to get her take on Will and what happened and whether she would be willing to write a short report with recommendations for Will's educational program. And fourth, I'd like Will to have a couple of evaluations."

"What kind of evaluations?"

"I'd like him to see a psychiatrist to see whether an expert would concur that Will has ADHD and to make programmatic recommendations. I'd also recommend an auditory-processing evaluation to determine whether Will has an auditory-processing disorder. Some of the comments I saw in the IEP led me to believe he might suffer from this condition."

"Whatever you say, Liz."

After Liz explained her fee structure and offered to answer Bill's questions, she pushed his records back toward him. "I'm sure you have a lot to think about. If you do decide to retain me, I'll want you to give me all the records you have on Will."

Bill looked stricken. "I do want to retain you. I'd like to get started immediately. I can't believe that the school has gotten away with this. Unfortunately, I'm on the verge of bankruptcy," he explained. "Is there any kind of payment plan you can put me on?"

"I'll take Will's case on a *pro bono* basis," Liz said.

"What does that mean?"

"All lawyers are required to do *pro bono* work, which means we take cases without accepting payment. Will's situation is compelling to me. I'd like to meet him. And since I believe you and the case is urgent, I'll get started right away."

Chapter Forty-Nine

After Bill had left the office, Liz recorded the pertinent facts of the case in preparation for contacting the school administration and its attorney. She was pissed off at the way yet another school district had improperly handled yet another kid with a disability—and motivated to get some relief for Will as soon as possible.

No matter how many cases Liz had handled, it never ceased to amaze her when she heard a story like Will's and encountered the utter failure of a school district to fulfill its obligation to a special needs student.

Conversely, Liz knew that there were dedicated staff in school districts. She had met them and worked with them on child study teams herself before becoming an attorney.

Sighing, Liz recalled Bill's comment that he had trusted the Child Study Team. She wished she had a dollar for every parent who'd said that, only to find out that their faith was misplaced.

With all those dollars, she thought, *I could start a legal fund to help parents who can't afford an attorney.* There were only so many *pro bono* clients Liz could manage every year. As an attorney, Liz was required to provide 25 hours per year to clients who could otherwise not afford legal representation. She often did triple or quadruple that amount, and it still wasn't enough to help all the people who couldn't afford her services.

Chapter Fifty

Outside Liz's office, Bill walked to his truck in a daze. Then, he sat in the Tahoe and cried. Liz Myler was an angel. When he had first seen her, her loveliness had momentarily distracted him from his purpose. But he was there for Will, so he'd shaken himself back into the present moment.

Now, here was Liz Myler, taking on Will's case for free. For the first time in a long time, Bill felt hope. He started the Tahoe and pointed it toward home, slowly working his way back through the concepts he and Liz had discussed. Having come for help with the criminal charges and their impact on Will's ability to play ball, it was hard to wrap his mind around the school district's probable failure to appropriately educate Will. His disbelief gave way to disgust, then anger.

He pictured Will's teachers, his case manager, the principal. *How could they have overlooked these huge responsibilities?* he wondered. *How could they have failed my son so grievously?* Following hard on the heels of these churning thoughts and emotions came anger toward himself, anger that he had missed what had happened before his very own eyes. He had failed his own son, his only remaining child. *How could I have missed it? And how could I have believed those teachers who told me Will was lazy? How can I ever forgive myself?*

Halfway home, Bill had an emotional revelation: He really *had* trusted the Child Study Team, and he should've been able to. They were the professionals charged with all those legal and educational duties. With Liz's help, they would fight back. And they would win.

Chapter Fifty-One

Will drove Troy to school on Tuesday morning. Both boys were in high spirits, and Will felt as if a score had been settled. The news hadn't reached the rest of the student body, so Troy had kept a low profile all day. He went to all his classes, but tried to stay out of sight of Will's friends. After last period, he met Will outside and they drove to the park to shoot some baskets. Although Troy waited anxiously for Will to tell him the good news, Will talked about everything but his legal problems.

Finally, Troy couldn't stand it any longer.

"Have you and your dad heard anything from the police?"

Will kept dribbling, his expression unreadable.

"Nothing yet."

Will stopped the ball mid-bounce and looked at Troy.

"Why'd you go to the police yesterday?"

Troy shrugged, embarrassed. In a voice barely above a whisper, he said, "After what you did for me?" He looked up into Will's face. "You saved my life. No one's ever done anything like that for me."

The boys continued shooting baskets, Will hopeful at the prospect of putting this all behind him now that the police knew he was innocent. Troy's relief at Will's happiness was short-lived, however. He still had to tell Will about Guzman, and how Guzman—and Ricky— had known where Will was last Tuesday. He forced himself to get it over with.

"Will, there's something else."

After he'd dropped the Guzman bomb and admitted he'd thrown Will to Guzman's mercy, the mood changed.

"Shit, Troy, that's a hell of a way to treat me after I fuckin' adopted you."

Will bounced the ball hard, jumped, and swished the ball through the net. Grabbing the rebound, he bounced it to Troy, hard. When Troy set up to shoot, Will jumped up and slapped the ball out of Troy's hands, swiveled, and pounded it into the hoop. Will monopolized Troy on the court for a few more rounds, then grabbed the ball and stood still.

"Troy, what's gonna happen when Guzman

comes back? I mean, he didn't get paid, right?"

When Troy just shrugged, Will quickly step-stepped across the court and got in Troy's face.

"You're gonna have to pay him. You gotta pay him, Troy, or you have to help the cops nail him."

Chapter Fifty-Two

Will was working at his desk at 6:00 p.m. when he heard the garage door open, announcing his father's arrival. He bounded down the stairs and met Bill in the kitchen. "How did it go?" he asked.

"It went well. I certainly got an education in the law," said Bill, stowing his keys. "I'll fill you in over dinner. But I hired the lawyer. Her name is Liz Myler. Actually, she offered to take your case for free. I think she'll be able to help with all the school-related issues."

"Wait, you don't have to pay her?"

"She wants to meet you first. She said if you are the kind of person I told her about, then, right, we don't have to pay."

"How come?"

"Because she thinks your case is 'compelling.'"

Will smiled. "And she can even help with basketball?"

"Even basketball." Bill smiled. "You'll have to do a few things to help the case." He explained the student appointment and the evaluations.

"Let's do it," said Will. "I'm ready. I'll go. I'll do whatever I have to do. I just want to put this behind me."

As Will lay in bed that night, reliving the day's highlights, memories of the attack began to slide into his awareness. He had a flashback of Ricky's false smile as he stepped onto the court, of Ricky asking Will if he wanted to get a game together.

Will put it out of his mind.

Time for sleeping, he thought. *Time to be positive and look forward to tomorrow and get this all cleared up.*

Will drifted off to sleep with a smile on his face. He dreamt of basketball games, friends slapping him on the back, and a full ride to college.

Chapter Fifty-Three

In the morning, Bill was at his desk feeling more lighthearted than he had in a long, long time. Now that Troy—maybe he wasn't such a dirt merchant after all—had gone to the police and told them the God's unvarnished truth, things were finally looking up for Will. So it was with a buoyant heart that he accepted a call from Declan Fennelly on his office landline.

"Declan, my man, good to hear from you," Bill nearly shouted into the phone. "What's the good word?"

Declan sighed. *Maybe I'll retire soon*, he thought. This was getting to be far too frustrating and savage a world.

"Bill, I'm sorry, but there is no good word. Not from this prosecutor."

"What? How is that possible? We've got a confession from the kid who actually did the crimes."

"I know it seems like Will's charges should all just disappear, but that's not how the law works. Will has been charged with conspiracy, so just because the Braithwaite kid confessed to being the main bad actor doesn't mean that Will might not be guilty of the crimes."

"But Troy explained to Detective Graham that Will knew nothing about the drugs."

"I know, I know. You've gotta look at it from their point of view. Will's older, smarter, and stronger than Troy. If you were the cops, what would *you* think? Is it the puny 16-year-old who was the mastermind here, or is it the brawny 18-year-old senior who was really doing the deals? And did Mr. Brawny threaten Mr. Puny that he'd better confess or else?"

"That's just ridiculous!" Bill exploded. "They don't know Will at all. And they're ignoring the evidence."

"You're right there. They don't know Will at all. Unfortunately, they now have conflicting evidence, and they're not going admit they were wrong and just wave a magic wand and make this all go away."

"What do we do now? Does Will still have to stand trial?"

"I hope not. I've got the next move lined up on the chessboard," Declan explained. "A summary judgment motion. It's a way to get this mix-up in front of the judge sooner rather than later. It will force the prosecutor to set forth all the evidence she's got against Will. If the judge rules in our favor, Will's case will be dismissed. It's a bit of a long shot, but it's worth a try now that we have Troy's confession."

"How soon can you file?"

Chapter Fifty-Four

Thursday morning found Will driving himself to Liz Myler's office for a ten o'clock appointment. The days hadn't gone fast enough for him; he had already missed almost two weeks of basketball practice.

Will's nervousness made him a little bouncy as he waited in the seating area to see her. He paced the room, looking at the books, the magazines on the table, never holding still, fingers stuck in his jean pockets. When she came to get him, he extended his right hand to shake hers, and she invited him back to the office.

Will followed her eagerly. He was well aware she might save him from the awful fate he couldn't bring himself to contemplate. He also responded well to women by virtue of the loss of his own mother and his own attraction to anything maternal. It gave him a puppy-dog-like charm that most women found endearing.

Liz Myler was no exception. However, as a

psychotherapist and an attorney, she was well-versed in analysis and in elevating her intellect over her emotions. But emotions were useful tools, and Liz tried to use them to her own, and her clients', benefit.

After she'd shut the door to her office and taken her seat, she had to urge Will to sit down, since he was still pacing, glancing around, taking in the details of her office.

"Will, do you know why I wanted you to come here today?"

Will, who hadn't ceased grinning since Liz had set eyes on him, answered, "To meet me."

"Well, yes, but why would I want to meet you?"

"Um, I'm not sure," Will replied, fidgeting in his seat, his gaze wandering around the office. "To make sure I'm the kind of person my dad told you about. Maybe to explain the law to me?"

"I've already explained that to your dad. Will," she said, and waited until he finally looked right at her.

"Are you nervous?"

He grinned sheepishly. "Maybe a little."

"You don't have to be nervous around me, Will. I'm here to help you. I just wanted to get to know you a little."

Switching gears while continuing the assessment she'd started the minute she'd opened the door to the waiting room, she asked, "Do you know what a licensed clinical social worker is?"

Will met her gaze. "My counselor is a licensed clinical social worker. At least, I think that's what she is."

"Judy Forrest, right?"

Will nodded.

"I'm also a licensed clinical social worker."

"I thought you were an attorney."

"I am. Before I became an attorney, I was already an LCSW. I worked with a lot of kids in psychotherapy in my private practice and in schools. I used to be on the Child Study Team in a couple different school districts. I helped students who had learning differences."

Will was now giving her all his attention and, it seemed, trust. Then, he dropped his gaze and looked down at his red Converse sneakers.

"I don't have learning differences. I have ADHD, but I'm just stupid sometimes."

Liz's heart clenched. "What makes you say that, Will?"

"I can never seem to get good grades. There's no way I could ever get an academic scholarship. And now I might not even get to go to college."

Liz took a breath, held it a minute, and waited. She had learned in graduate school how to "sit" with a client while they confronted painful realities. That was one reason she waited. The other, more important, reason, however, was that she wasn't Will's psychotherapist; she was Will's lawyer. She had no wish to cross that line. So, she waited and assessed. And her motherly heart hurt for this motherless boy-man. "Will," she asked, "do you have a disability?"

"Yes, if ADHD is a disability."

"Can you tell me the symptoms of ADHD you experience?"

He fidgeted in his chair and twisted his hands together, picking under his fingernails. "Well, I never remember anything, and I get distracted really easily." He paused, bouncing his right leg and staring into space.

"Anything else?"

Will looked back at her. "What?" he asked.

"Do you have other symptoms besides never remembering anything?"

"Oh, yeah. Um, I have a hard time with big projects and writing papers. I can never figure out how or where to start or how to organize anything."

"Do you think that ADHD affects your educational performance?"

Will considered the question for a moment. "Yeah."

"Do you know what your IQ is?"

"Yeah, I got tested in school, and then Judy went over my tests with me and explained it all."

"So what does your IQ say about you?"

"Um, I have a high average IQ."

"So, given everything that you've just told me, Will, are you stupid?"

Will cast his gaze at the floor and answered her quietly, "No."

"That's the right answer." Liz smiled at Will. "So tell me about basketball," she said.

Will grinned at her, instantly happy again. "What do you wanna know?"

Chapter Fifty-Five

Twenty minutes later, after Will left her office smiling again, full of life and energy, Liz sent out a couple of emails to the experts she had in mind. She wanted to get the evaluations done ASAP and get Will back in school with a program that would really work for him. It was his senior year, after all, and he didn't have that much time left to learn basic study skills and compensatory strategies to handle his ADHD in college.

Next, she wrote to the school district, advising that she represented both William Van Dalen, Sr., and his son, William Van Dalen, Jr., regarding the free, appropriate public education the district was required to provide. She noted that the district had suspended Will for 15 school days for conduct off of school grounds without holding the requisite manifestation determination review. By failing to provide this procedural safeguard, she wrote, the district was violating Will's civil rights and placing him in danger of irreparable harm: the loss of his basketball scholarship. Liz also detailed the deficiencies she'd found in the IEP, and noted that, due to these deficiencies alone, the district had violated Will's rights by failing to provide FAPE. For those reasons, Liz demanded that a meeting be held within 48 hours, at which the district would consider and make revisions to Will's IEP and allow him to return to school. She had her assistant wing this document to the district and its attorney via email for immediate notice and response.

Then, Liz picked up the phone and called the school district's special ed attorney, Paul Kingston. Lawyers get a lot accomplished talking with one another outside the hearing of their clients. After all, they both know what the law requires, and they have a good idea who had complied with it and who hadn't.

In this case, with a high-profile news story involving a local basketball star, a kidnapping charge, and a divided town, getting down to brass tacks regarding the requirements of the law was only the first step. Next, a successful outcome would require immediate pressure through threat of litigation and movement through that process so the school district could understand its responsibility to Will and step up to the plate.

The problem here, thought Liz, *is that Will doesn't have time to move through the process in the usual time frame.* Cases often took nine to 12 months to resolve. If they went to trial, it might take two years. If the losing party appealed, add another 18 months. No, Will Van Dalen needed immediate results.

She picked up the phone and dialed the number she knew by memory. She often joked that she had her adversaries' numbers on speed dial. The special ed bar was a specialized group of attorneys and consisted of only a handful of practitioners. They all knew each other and saw each other regularly as adversaries and, Liz believed, colleagues.

Paul answered his cell phone on the first ring with a crisp, clear greeting. When Liz explained Will's circumstances, and the district's failures, to him, he immediately went on the offensive.

"Liz, get real. You can't expect my client to let this kid back into school. After what he did? I'm gonna send him to our psychiatrist, and we'll get support to keep him out till the end of the year. Then we'll graduate him, and he won't be our problem anymore."

"Paul, with a 15-day suspension, your client is past time to hold the manifestation determination meeting. You'd better have them convene a meeting right away. They're already in violation of state and federal law. If they hold a meeting tomorrow or Monday, I'll agree not to file for emergent relief. Why don't you talk to your client and get back to me today and we'll firm up a date?"

Despite his initial bluster, Paul acquiesced. He knew that his client had screwed up, and it was time to step in to try and prevent things from getting worse.

Chapter Fifty-Six

O fficer Brandt's duty boots rang on the tile as he strode down the internal hallway of the police station. Seeing Detective Graham at his desk, Brandt stopped by with an update.

"Hey, Graham. Good news. We picked up both perps from the attack on the Van Dalen kid. Charged them with the whole nine yards: possession, intent to sell, illegal possession of a firearm, aggravated assault, and conspiracy."

"That *is* good news. Yeah, Troy surprised me yesterday when he came back with the rest of the story. Maybe there's hope for that kid yet. But it was definitely the break we needed to catch Guzman. Hey, listen to this: Troy even came in with a lawyer who wants to negotiate a deal that keeps Troy out of juvie."

"He's got a lawyer?"

"Yeah, Declan Fennelly came in with him."

"No shit!"

"He's gonna have to testify, though, so we can nail these guys."

Brandt laughed.

"I don't think that'll be necessary. The little guy, Ricky? He's squealing like a pig. We've got plenty of evidence against Guzman now."

Chapter Fifty-Seven

By Thursday evening, Liz had heard back from both the audiologist and the psychiatrist she'd contacted. Both agreed to squeeze Will in immediately. Liz picked up the phone and called Bill, impressing on him that both experts had agreed to see Will over the weekend and he should contact both of them as soon as he hung up to make the appointments.

Earlier that afternoon, Paul Kingston had called Liz in the office. He and the district agreed to hold the meeting as soon as possible, on Monday morning. Once they ended their brief call, Liz telephoned Bill to prepare him for what might happen at the meeting, and together they agreed to follow the advice of Will's counselor and keep him from attending. He wasn't in any kind of position psychologically to withstand the type of discussion that might occur behind closed doors under these circumstances.

Will had both evaluations done over the weekend, and Liz received the reports via email. Bill cleared her to send them immediately to board counsel with a "demand" letter. In the letter, Liz advised that Will had been evaluated by both an audiologist and a psychiatrist, and that he had been diagnosed with depression, anxiety, ADHD, and an auditory processing disorder. Given the needs created by these conditions, both experts had reviewed Will's IEP and found it inappropriate to meet his special needs. She concluded by asking Paul to review with the school district prior to the meeting so the reports could be used to help plan Will's educational program.

Chapter Fifty-Eight

On Monday morning, Liz met Bill in front of the Ocean Beach Board of Education Administrative Offices. It was a glorious mid-autumn day with a snap in the air, and the trees were a riot of vivid colors. Despite the beauty of the day, Bill looked gaunt and haggard when he arrived. Shadows under his sunken eyes revealed the internal ravages of his own suffering at the hands of the school district.

"Good morning, Bill."

His wry smile looked more like a grimace. "Is it? I hadn't noticed." Then he said, sheepishly, "Sorry. I'm not a pessimist by nature. This whole thing has been such a nightmare."

"As I always say, run to the roar."

Startled, Bill stared at her. "That's what Will used to say. Before all this happened."

"Let that be a good omen, then. Unless you have questions, I suggest we head on inside and get this party started."

"I'm with you, counselor."

After Liz and Bill signed in at the front desk, the receptionist buzzed the conference room, and Will's case manager greeted them and lead them to the meeting. As they entered, Liz saw that the conference table was full of school officials and staff members— 12 in all—a literal show of force.

Liz and Bill said their hellos as they shuffled in and found seats at the table, aware of the eyes on them.

The case manager started the meeting as if the district itself had arranged it and it was simply business as usual. The teachers reported Will's PLAAFP, explaining how he was doing in all of his subjects.

Liz was surprised that the district was proceeding as if they had arranged this meeting, but she kept quiet. *After all*, she reasoned, *if they want to address Will's IEP and get him back to school with changes that help him obtain the meaningful educational benefit to which he's entitled, I won't argue.*

The learning-disabilities teacher and consultant, Mr. D'Angelo, a specially trained teacher called an LDT/C for short, was present and agreed with Liz's written recommendation that Will needed an organizational coach, instruction in organizational strategies, and some one-on-one instruction in some of his academics. The LDT/C advised he could do all of that during the last period of the day so Will would be organized each day before he left the school building. Mr. D'Angelo could also coordinate with a special education teacher who would act as in-class support in Will's core curriculum subjects. That would provide Will with specialized assistance if he needed it. The special ed teacher would "chunk" his assignments, breaking down the difficult parts into more manageable pieces, then teach Will how to start and complete his work independently.

During these pronouncements, Liz caught Paul Kingston's eye across the table. From the friendly demeanor and cooperative attitude with which she and Bill were received at this meeting, she knew that Paul must have used her letter to spearhead some intensive discussions with these school officials. He would have used the citations of law and the failures detailed in the letter to read them the riot act and explain what might happen if they ignored their obligations to Will. She saw the ghost of a smile flit across his face, but if she hadn't been watching closely and didn't know him so well, she would have questioned her own eyesight.

Internally, Liz had mixed feelings as she listened to the various staff members happily reporting the accommodations and modifications they would provide Will in his educational program.

Why didn't they do this years ago? she wondered

angrily. It was their duty, their legal responsibility to evaluate Will in all areas of suspected disability. It was so obvious that he needed these types of supports that anyone could have seen it, even upon a cursory review.

Ever practical, Liz reasoned that they were, on the other hand, responding appropriately to her push in the right direction. Will deserved compensation for the years of the district's failure to provide FAPE, but after her discussion with both Bill and Will, she knew the goal was to get Will back in school and playing basketball immediately.

When Vin Flowers, the superintendent, announced that they'd be happy to welcome Will back to school and the basketball team, Bill turned to look at her, dumbfounded.

Liz smiled at him, then turned to look at Vin Flowers and the director of special services. "Are you all in agreement, then, that Will can return to practice this afternoon?"

The 12 team members turned to face her, momentarily speechless.

Liz seized the moment. "Let me be completely forthright with you. While Will and Mr. Van Dalen appreciate these changes to Will's IEP, we have yet to discuss the district's actions in suspending Will without the appropriate manifestation determination.

You violated Will's rights in that regard. It's my legal opinion," she continued, looking Vin Flowers and the director dead in the eye, "that Will should not have been suspended in the first place. The law required several actions here, all of which you failed to perform. That's why we believe he must return immediately."

Here, she paused and looked at the school's attorney, who was rolling his pen furiously through his fingers. "Shall Mr. Van Dalen and I step out and give you time to discuss our request?"

Paul smiled tightly. "That would be a good idea."

Liz nodded at Bill. They rose simultaneously from their chairs, stepped out into the hallway, and found a quiet alcove where Liz was sure they could confer privately.

"What's going on?" Bill asked.

"So far, so good," Liz replied. "They're agreeing to appropriate modifications and accommodations for Will's IEP. They also know they need to cover their backsides and get Will back to school, so things are moving in the right direction. However," she added, "they still needed a little push so Will can return immediately."

"Do you think we're pushing too much at this point? I mean, they are agreeing he can come back."

"No. Will has every right to be in school and playing basketball. We need to get closure now. Otherwise, we could get delayed, and we'll get no benefit out of this meeting."

Bill shoved his hands into his trouser pockets and took a firm stance. "I'll take your word for it."

A few moments later, Paul poked his head out of the conference room and beckoned to them.

As Liz took her seat at the table, she took stock of each staff member. *It's like trying to read the jury when you return for the verdict,* she thought. *You get a sense of which way things are going by assessing the amount of time it took for those 12 citizens to render a verdict and the body language of each juror.* Liz was happy to see the district folks looking comfortable, happy, even magnanimous. That meant there was no conflict and there would be no opposition to her request.

True to her internal prediction, Vin Flowers, ever the statesman, addressed Liz and Bill with a flourish.

"If Will is prepared to return to school this afternoon, he can attend seventh and eighth period. For today only, he will meet with the LDT/C for those two periods and the LDT/C will help Will assess where he is with his assignments. He will also outline a plan to help him catch up with his classes. Will can then attend basketball practice after school.

After today, he'll return to his normal schedule subject to the modifications of his IEP."

In an effort to exclude Liz, Vin looked at Bill and asked, "Is that agreeable to you, Mr. Van Dalen?"

Before Bill could respond, Liz said, "Mr. Van Dalen has advised me he is agreeable to the proposed IEP subject to a more thorough review after this meeting. He has expressed his wish that Will return to school and to practice today, so yes, Mr. Van Dalen is in agreement with your proposal."

She paused, looking at each staff member in turn. She knew how important it was for people to save face and to be recognized for doing the right thing, even if they did it late. At least it wasn't *too* late.

"On behalf of Will and his father, I want to say thank you for revising Will's IEP so he can resume his studies and his basketball activities right away. I think you know that this can make Will's future, instead of breaking it."

Liz and Bill offered their thanks, said their good-byes, and shook hands all around.

When they stepped out into the waiting room, they found Will seated in a chair. He stood at their approach.

Before Bill or Liz could speak, he blurted out, "Dad, don't be mad. I just had to find out what happened. I couldn't get anything done this morning knowing you were at this meeting."

Bill laid a hand on Will's shoulder and smiled into his face. "That's okay, Will. I'm not angry."

Before he could continue, Will asked, "What happened? Am I still suspended?"

Bill glanced at Liz. She smiled encouragement. "You tell him," she said.

"You're going back to school and to basketball practice this afternoon,"

Will stared back at Bill in disbelief. "Are you kidding me? Really, Dad, *really*?" A million-watt grin split his face. "I have to go in and say thank you. Is everyone still in the room? Is that okay?"

Liz and Bill exchanged a look. "I think that's a great idea, Will," said Liz. "Come on."

The trio walked down the hall to the conference room door where Liz rapped three times to announce them. As she opened the door, she announced, "Incoming," in case the school group members were discussing details they did not want her to hear. "Will's here," she announced. "He has something to say." She opened the door wide to admit Will.

Will came in wearing a pair of jeans, his signature red Converse sneakers, and letter jacket. He was beaming as he went to Superintendent Flowers. As he extended his hand, he said, "Sir, I just wanted to say thank you for letting me come back to school."

He went from Dr. Flowers to the director of special services to the case manager to the teachers and all the other participants, grinning and shaking hands, all the while streaming heartfelt thanks. He was so obviously sincere, so happy, that his mood was infectious, and the whole crowd responded to him.

And a little bit of magic happened, Liz thought. *The magic that occurs when humans fulfill the spirit of the law and it changes the course of human life.*

Afterward, Liz lingered on the sidewalk with father and son. Bill was still agog, Will still beaming.

"I can't believe this is happening," Bill said to Liz. "I can't get over it. This is such an about-face from just 11 days ago, when Declan called the principal. This wouldn't have happened if it weren't for you."

Embarrassed in the face of such frank praise, Liz downplayed her role as heroine. "That's my job, and Declan is doing his job, too. He's Will's criminal attorney, so he'll handle things from that end for you."

"It's hard to wrap my mind around it still," Bill continued. "I can't even think straight. Is there anything I'm missing? What else do we need to do?"

Liz smiled. "I think Will needs to get home and gather up his books so he can get to school by seventh period." She added: "It may be hard to walk in there, Will. You may hear some ugly things from some people, like that guy in Joey's. Do you know how you'll handle that?"

Looking down, Will kicked his toe against the curb and shrugged his shoulders slightly. He looked back up at Liz. "Maybe I'll just take things one day at a time, like Judy says. Run to the roar if I have to."

The breeze kicked up just them, sending a shower of brilliant yellow leaves swirling around them.

"How do you do that, Will?"

"It'll depend on what happens. If the other kids say things to me, I might ignore that. If one of the guys on the team mouths off to me, that might be something different."

"How?"

"I might try to catch him alone and speak to him man-to-man." Will had no idea how young he looked at that moment with the direct sunlight revealing his smooth features. But something new glinted in his eye: Will Van Dalen had learned new and unforgettable lessons, not in a classroom, but from experience.

"Sounds like a plan," Liz said.

After talking with the Van Dalens briefly about

the steps they would each need to take to finalize the work they had done together, Liz walked to her car for the drive back to the office, back to the files of all the other students who needed her. Thanks to the twin nemeses of ignorance and greed, Liz's work was never done. She smiled wryly to herself. *Good thing we didn't listen to Shakespeare and kill all the lawyers.*

Chapter Fifty-Nine

Declan Fennelly strode purposefully out of the sprawling courthouse in Toms River after filing his summary judgment motion. To say he felt relieved was an understatement. He had worked all weekend on that damned motion, and even now, he began mentally re-reviewing all of the points.

It's a lawyer's habit to review and review and review again to make sure they didn't miss a point, a fact, a potential pitfall. A lawyer must imagine "the Parade of Horribles"—think Murphy's Law on steroids—then plan ahead to avoid any of the horrors that might befall one's client. You must dance, and dance well. Otherwise, you may get sued for malpractice.

And we can't have that, can we? thought Declan. After all, a lawyer's mainstay is reputation, reputation, reputation.

Declan gave himself a mental shake. He had turned himself inside out on this particular case, and wondered whether he hadn't made a mistake in representing his own godchild.

I love that boy to the moon and back, he thought.

There was an old legal adage: *Never represent yourself or you'll have a fool for a client.* That principle carried over to family and friends. In law school, they warned that the ties that bind are the ties that blind.

Declan laughed to himself. *Everyone does it at some time or another. How do you say no to someone you love who's down on their luck?*

Speaking of which, Declan was well aware that Bill's business was going down the tubes, and he wished there was more he could do.

But I can do this, he thought, *and this might make all the difference.* Since Carolyn and Patrick had been killed in the train wreck, Bill and Will had seemed frozen—Bill especially. He tried to send business Bill's way, but the word he heard through his business associates and contacts in the community was that Bill had come undone. He was just going through the motions.

Declan had visited them on weekends, taken Bill out for coffee, given both of them pep talks he knew weren't doing any good. When he suggested to Bill that Bill start dating again, he thought Bill would give him a solid fist to the jaw for his concern.

"I've got Will to think about," he snapped, glaring at Declan. "And I'm too busy with the business to even think about that, anyway."

Declan also thought Bill felt too miserable and guilty about surviving his wife and youngest son, but he wisely kept his mouth shut after the dating fiasco.

Then this crisis had struck, and he sure as hell wasn't going to charge Bill for wanting him to look out for his godson. Bill would just have to swallow his pride and deal with it. With his business on the verge of going under, he'd have no choice.

Chapter Sixty

Will got a warm welcome at school from most of the teachers and student body. When he heard muttering in the corners, he kept his head down and ignored it.

He met with the LDT/C, Mr. D'Angelo, who was cheerful, upbeat, and made organization seem simple with color-coded everything. Mr. D'Angelo coordinated with all of Will's teachers to ensure he and Will had a comprehensive plan of the work Will needed to do. Mr. D'Angelo also made a plan with Will that they'd meet every afternoon during last period until Will got caught up with his assignments. Finally, he taught Will how to break down larger assignments into smaller tasks and how to write and organize a research paper.

Instead of all of this being daunting, Will was dazzled and felt much more competent. For his part, Mr. D'Angelo was pleased to learn how bright Will actually was and how readily he plunged into the work. All he'd needed was a little guidance and the right methods.

On his first afternoon back in school, Will had made it clear to his teammates that Troy was his unofficial little brother and not to be tampered with. He shared with them some of the shittier aspects of Troy's life, and that Troy had shown courage and integrity by going back to the police station to make a full confession. He explained that Troy had even agreed to testify against Guzman if necessary. The boys were impressed and agreed that, from now on, they'd let Troy be. Will had invited Troy to basketball practice and talked Coach Lichtenberg into making Troy the team's manager—whatever that meant. Will just wanted Troy to be part of something, to help him stay out of trouble, and to help Troy meet his obligations under his agreement with the prosecutor's office. He didn't care what they called it. He and Coach had put together a list of things for Troy to do to keep him busy and exposed to positive activities and good role models.

Troy was put in charge of setting up all of the equipment and water for the players. He started attending home games and riding the bus to away games. After a few weeks, he even began to assist the coach by giving directions during drills.

Chapter Sixty-One

After getting caught back up in the whirlwind of schoolwork and basketball practice, Will had almost forgotten about the criminal charges against him. Bill had not. He knew that the court wouldn't hear or decide upon Declan's summary judgment motion for about three weeks. He tried tucking it away in the back of his mind, but it sat there like a ticking time bomb.

In the meantime, he had another bomb to defuse— the impending demise of his business. After Liz Myler had gotten Will back into school—miraculously, in Bill's opinion—Bill was so juiced that he sat down and drew up a business plan to bring his company back from the brink.

Bankruptcy was an absolute last resort. He had started his business from scratch and had put his heart and soul into it. If he had done it once, he could do it again. By God, he could at least try. He owed it to Will, to Carolyn and Patrick.

The whole thing was very humbling. He had a team meeting with his two managers, then a company-wide conference. He apologized for letting things go. He asked for their help in getting through the next rough patch and promised them that if they stuck by him, they would become shareholders in the company. He had contracts drawn up for all of them to that effect. At first, he warned, there would be some painful belt-tightening, starting with a 10 percent pay cut, which would last for a year. It was the only way out.

"I'm not asking you to do anything I'm not doing," Bill explained.

He showed them all of the figures so everything was transparent.

He advised those who planned to stay that they were taking a risk and gambling on him. He outlined his plan to approach all of the customers who had terminated business with Van Dalen Lumber & Landscaping to see whether he could win them back, including Harrington-Davis.

Bill also shared his ideas for branching out the commercial and residential landscaping sections of the company. He'd been in touch with local vocational schools and had negotiated a deal wherein the senior carpentry and horticulture students would work as unpaid interns. In return, Bill and his managers would provide supervision, teaching them valuable skills and doing the paperwork so they could earn 15 credits a semester.

All in all, Bill thought, this could really work. The employees agreed and vowed to stick by him.

In a strange way, Will's legal crisis had brought Bill back to reality after years of living in a fog.

And I have one person, especially, to thank for it, he thought.

The beautiful, intelligent, and kind lady-lawyer, Liz Myler. He'd made up his mind to ask her out on a date. He wanted to rub his hands together in anticipation—even though they were clammy with apprehension. After all, he hadn't dated in over 20 years. *Was it like riding a bike?* he wondered. *Once you learned, could you get right back on and you'd find your balance was right there waiting for you?*

He was about to find out.

Chapter Sixty-Two

"Liz Myler."

The direct way she answered her phone made him tingle. He had a sudden urge to hang up so he wouldn't embarrass himself. *Grow up, Van Dalen,* he thought. *You can do this.*

"Hi, Liz, it's Bill Van Dalen."

After the initial pleasantries were exchanged, there was an unspoken question in the air. Bill grabbed the opportunity and said, "I have an ulterior motive for calling."

"Ulterior motives can be intriguing. How can I help?"

"Uh, for starters, you could agree to have coffee with me."

Coffee was harmless enough. You sat in a café in broad daylight. It didn't have to take long, or you could linger over it, maybe order a second cup. The conversation could be light and sweet, like the coffee, or it could go a little deeper.

It went a little deeper. Bill was a pretty handsome and intelligent guy, too. It wasn't too painful for the lovely Liz Myler to watch Bill's eyes twinkle over coffee or exchange laughs with him as they walked along the Ocean Beach Boardwalk, even in the chill November breezes. As Thanksgiving approached, Bill got up the courage to invite Liz over for dinner.

"What can I bring?" she asked.

Chapter Sixty-Three

The turkey, nestled among roasted Brussels sprouts, carrots, and pearl onions, came out golden brown. The table groaned under the weight of two kinds of sweet potatoes (baked and candied), cranberry sauce, mashed potatoes, and rolls. Bill, Will, Liz, Aunt Dana, her husband, Sam, their sons, Richard and Michael, Declan Fennelly, and Troy Braithwaite himself gathered around the feast.

Carl Braithwaite had agreed to a 28-day stay in rehab. Troy's brother, Marc, had to work until four at the pizza parlor, where they were roasting turkeys for the needy in the ovens. He'd swing by later for dessert, courtesy of Liz Myler, who had brought homemade pumpkin and deep-dish apple pies, along with whipped cream.

The party was jolly and festive. The prospects for Bill's business had improved. After hearing Bill's backstory and business plan, Robert Harrington had agreed to bring his lumber business back to Bill on a trial basis.

Will thought that was hilarious. "You're on parole, and I'm not!" He laughed gleefully.

Bill's idea of using the senior vo-tech students at Van Dalen Landscaping & Lumber had been genius. The students were knowledgeable in plant science, landscape design, and construction, and could be sent out on jobs like any other employee. Instead of getting a paycheck, however, they earned credits. The increase in revenue from their contributions would help move the company's bottom line from red to black over the next year. If business continued to improve, it looked as if Bill would be able to give his loyal employees a raise by then.

Will had his own good news to share, which added to the air of thanksgiving. Since he'd been back to school, several college coaches had seen him play ball. They had been duly impressed, and he had received four offers to play basketball in return for his full tuition. Will was considering the offers, but he was leaning toward Rutgers, the State University of New Jersey.

Much talk and laughter ensued from all this good news. If Declan was a little quieter than usual, no one noticed. He had one thing on his mind: Next Friday, Judge Giordano would hear Declan's summary judgment motion. It wasn't worth discussing at this holiday table since there was nothing more to be said at the moment. It was all speculation until the judge made his ruling. So Declan smiled and ate, helped clear the table, and cheered on his football team while eating pie with the gang.

Chapter Sixty-Four

Fridays are usually motion days in court, and this Friday, the first motion day in December, was no different. The courtroom was hushed as the assembly awaited Judge Giordano's arrival. Small attorney-client clusters were scattered throughout the courtroom, where hushed, last-minute conferences took place. Both warnings and encouragement were doled out.

Declan had approached the judge's clerk to let him know he was present. He had requested oral argument, but that guaranteed exactly nothing.

There was a general stirring as the court clerk leapt to his feet and announced, "All rise!"

The tall figure of Hugo-to-Hell swept into the courtroom and up to his bench, black robes swirling around him. "Please be seated," he commanded. After he booted up his computer, he announced, "Court is now in session."

Declan grew almost bored as the judge dealt with

the easier motions, which helped clear the courtroom. But when he intoned, "State v. Van Dalen," Declan was alert and on his feet.

"Defendant is ready, Your Honor."

After establishing that both parties were present, Judge Giordano addressed Declan.

"Mr. Fennelly, I understand that you have requested oral argument." He looked down from his bench directly at Declan. "However, after reading your motion and Ms. Foster's opposition, I do not believe oral argument is necessary. Let me tell you why.

"It is obvious—crystal clear is what you attorneys are always telling me—that Mr. Van Dalen knew nothing about the purpose of stopping at the Sullivan home the night of October 23rd. He was simply doing a favor for a friend. When he put his car in drive, the door locks engaged automatically. There was no nefarious intent and no *mens rea*; therefore, it is not possible that Mr. Van Dalen committed the crime of kidnapping. Further, when he realized what was going on in the back seat of his car, he pulled immediately to the curb and freed the Sullivan boy, who proceeded to hightail it home. All of the attached signed witness statements concur on these points."

The judge turned to look at the prosecutor. "At

this time, we have a signed confession from Mr. Braithwaite to this effect, admitting that he was at fault and that he had initially lied to protect himself. Isn't that true, Ms. Foster?"

The prosecutor stood to address His Honor. "Yes, Judge, but Troy Braithwaite is a minor. It is entirely possible that Mr. Van Dalen put pressure on Troy, perhaps even threatened him, to force him to give this confession. The prosecution believes—"

Judge Giordano cut her off before she could get further. He raised his eyebrows and, eyes boring into hers, asked, "Just what proof do you have of such action? None was offered in your opposition."

"At this time the prosecution has no tangible evidence that Mr. Van Dalen threatened Troy, Your Honor. However, given time—"

"You talk about time? How about not wasting the court's time with this case when the defendant who actually committed the crimes confessed to them? Tell me, Ms. Foster, did you read the entirety of Mr. Fennelly's papers?"

"Yes, Your Honor."

"Based on the argument set forth in your papers and here this morning, I wasn't sure. And did that include Mr. Braithwaite's affidavit, wherein he set forth the actual reasons he decided to come down to the police station and make this sworn statement?"

The prosecutor seemed to shrink a little from the judge's withering tone. "Yes, Your Honor."

"And you saw that those reasons included that Mr. Van Dalen has been like a brother to him? And that he himself set the drug dealer onto Mr. Van Dalen, who was then attacked in the local park, an attack which sent him to the emergency room via ambulance? And that, even after all that provocation, Mr. Van Dalen saved Mr. Braithwaite from jumping in front of a North Jersey Coast Line train and taking his own life?"

The prosecutor hung her head. "Yes, Your Honor."

"Perhaps you might reconsider whether your office would like to drop the charges against Mr. Van Dalen rather than having me put my thoughts into a lengthy judicial decision."

"Would Your Honor grant us a five-minute recess?"

It might have been even fewer than five minutes that passed before the prosecutor came back and declared, on the record, that the prosecutor's office was dropping all charges against William Van Dalen, Jr.

Chapter Sixty-Five

There was jubilation in the house that night, and the same Thanksgiving crowd assembled to ring in the good news. It was Friday night, Pizza Night, but tonight it was a celebration on steroids. Bill and Will were over the moon, Bill slapping Declan Fennelly on the back and making toasts.

Troy was there, too, although he was a little quiet until Declan shared with him the chat he'd had with the prosecutor on Troy's behalf. The prosecutor had agreed that, due to Troy's life circumstances and the cooperation he'd demonstrated, he could avoid a trial or even a plea bargain if he would agree to certain conditions. Troy would have to do 100 hours of community service, he'd have to stay out of trouble until he graduated from high school, and he'd have to make restitution to the Sullivan family.

Declan glanced at Liz, grateful for her educational input that helped him get creative with Troy's community service. Troy would work off his hours in the vo-tech program with Van Dalen Lumber &

Landscaping. The "restitution" wouldn't be monetary; the Sullivans had elected to have Troy do work around their house and yard, supervised by Joe Sullivan himself, with Ryan joining in after the first two months. The Sullivans, who had learned about Troy's home life, believed in second chances, and they wanted to show their boys an example of making positive change in the world.

As they each took turns sharing their good news, another cheer would go up. The relief in the room was visible; you could see it on each shining face: Will, jubilant, beaming at everyone; Bill, relieved and unburdened; Troy, sort of shy and sort of hopeful, looking around at all these people and wondering how his world had changed for the better so quickly; Liz, looking content about each piece of this puzzle coming together; and Declan, proud of his godson and relieved that the whole ordeal was over.

Holy shit, thought Troy, looking at all the happy faces and exhilarated by the good feelings coursing through him. He looked at Will again. *I almost threw all of this away.*

Afterword

The themes of family, forgiveness, and redemption are important in life. After all, who among us goes through life without making a mistake? And who does not need some support and encouragement from time to time?

The twining of these three cords in the lives of teens and vulnerable adults can help stem the epidemic of suicide which has erupted in our nation. You can do your part by simply being aware of those around you. Is there anyone you know who might be fragile, who has suffered significant loss? Ask them how they're doing. Meet up and go for a walk. Grab a cup of coffee. Make room, with your own silence, for them to talk. Listen.

Remember that suicide is a permanent solution to a temporary problem. If you or anyone you know has thoughts of suicide, please call the National Suicide Prevention Lifeline at 1-800-273-8255. Save a life today.

For years, Jayne M. Wesler worked with students after they attempted suicide or homicide or both. She also represented them in the legal arena, ensuring that kids with disabilities got appropriate educational programs as required by state and federal law. This enabled most of them to have comprehensive and fulfilling lives. The vast majority of the students in both settings, especially the locked psychiatric unit, did not really want to die; they just didn't have the tools to find their own way.

Other books by Jayne Wesler

HANDBOOK FOR PARENTS OF CHILDREN WITH SPECIAL NEEDS: A THERAPEUTIC AND LEGAL APPROACH

As a lawyer, psychotherapist, and former Child Study Team member who practiced exclusively on behalf of children with special needs, Jayne Wesler has helped hundreds, if not thousands, of parents obtain educational programs which led to their child's success. In this book, she shares information with you from federal and state law, federal and state regulations, psychotherapeutic techniques, and her experience so that you, too, can change the trajectory of your child's life. If you use the techniques, tools, and knowledge she provides to you, you can and will obtain successful programs for your child to help them succeed in school—the sooner, the better.

Children grow so quickly that, when they do need help, they need it immediately. Don't wait. Do it today. You'll be glad you did.

"This book is an easy-to-read, go-to manual containing pearls of wisdom and accessible references for creating your child's educational blueprint. Jayne Wesler created this handbook blending both wisdom and heart!"

Jill Brooks, PhD, clinical neuropsychologist, Head 2 Head Consulting

"With her background as a psychotherapist and an education attorney, Jayne Wesler has written a thoughtful and practical guide for parents of children with special needs looking to navigate the sometimes turbulent and confusing waters of the special education world."

Daniel DaSilva, PhD, pediatric neuropsychologist, Morris Psychological Group

"This is an essential guide for parents seeking the best education for their children, important information from an expert attorney, educator, and psychotherapist. A must-read."

Ellen Fenster-Kuehl, PhD, licensed psychologist

"The book you hold in your hand is a blueprint to navigating the complexities of educational programming. Attorney and psychotherapist Jayne Wesler integrates her knowledge and offers a unique perspective on how to truly transform your child's life."

Melissa Fiorito-Grafman, PhD, clinical neuropsychologist, Center for Neuropsychology & Psychotherapy

"Attorney and psychotherapist Jayne Wesler shares her practical knowledge on how to truly transform your child's life."

Dana Henning, EdD, education consultant, Dana Henning Training Programs

Available on Amazon.com

Walmart.com

BarnesandNoble.com

HURTS SO GOOD
AN ORGASM OF TEARS

Have you ever had a good cry? Maybe it is rare for you, or maybe it happens at the drop of a hat.

Have you ever wondered about the biology of tears?

Have you ever noticed the physical aspects of your emotional tears? Quivering abs? The prick of tears in your eyes? Chest tightening? Throat hurting? Nostrils flaring? Mouth crumpling?

Have you ever been scolded or criticized for crying?

Would it intrigue you to know that there are significant similarities between emotional tears and orgasm?

Join me to delve into this most baffling of human behaviors: the shedding of emotional tears or, as we know it in the vernacular, a "good cry."

Jayne Wesler has played many roles in her life. From the newsroom to the intense hush of psychotherapy sessions in various venues, including a locked psychiatric unit in a large urban hospital, to trying cases in courtrooms in Newark, Trenton, and Atlantic City, New Jersey, Ms. Wesler has been both witness to and actor in the most intense of human dramas. Trained by experts at GCU and NYU to use her emotions as a tool, Ms. Wesler is able to tap into human experience to help educate and heal others. In this riveting expose, Ms. Wesler illuminates the parallels between orgasm and emotional tears, thereby demonstrating a biological legitimacy to the need for a good cry. Just as sex is the all-time, one-and-only treatment for epididymal hypertension, commonly known as "blue balls," a good cry is the only remedy for a frustrated and achy soul—a blue heart.

Available on Amazon.com

Walmart.com

BarnesandNoble.com

HURTS SO GOOD:
AN ORGASM OF TEARS
WORKBOOK

Learn how to deepen your most important relationships with exercises for emotional intimacy. This workbook is the companion to *Hurts So Good: An Orgasm of Tears*. You will be surprised how much your trust and your love for yourself and your partner will deepen when you utilize the activities and exercises in this extraordinary book.

My tears are my gift to you.

They mean I trust you; I am making myself vulnerable to you; I am opening myself up to you; I am taking the risk of being hurt to deepen my bonds with you. Maybe even I love you.

Available on Amazon.com

Walmart.com

BarnesandNoble.com

NO BONES ABOUT IT:

HOW TO INCREASE YOUR BONE DENSITY WITHOUT MEDICATION

The purpose of this book is to reach the millions of women and men who are diagnosed with bone loss and to give them—and maybe you, dear Reader—a viable alternative to taking medication to increase their bone density.

Have you gotten a diagnosis of osteopenia or osteoporosis? Has someone you love been diagnosed? If you are freaking out and wondering what you can do, take a deep breath. **There are steps you can take to strengthen your bones**. This diagnosis does not define your life. Open this book and keep reading to learn how you can assess your risk factors, summon and utilize your resources, and make positive changes in the health of your bones.

Available on Amazon.com

Walmart.com

BarnesandNoble.com

Jayne M. Wesler is an author, coach, speaker, licensed clinical social worker, and attorney. She is the author of *Handbook for Parents of Children with Special Needs: A Therapeutic and Legal Approach; Hurts So Good: An Orgasm of Tears; Hurts So Good: An Orgasm of Tears Workbook; No Bones About It: Increase Your Bone Density Without Medication*; and the novel *Railroaded.* Ms. Wesler, a partner in the law firm of Sussan, Greenwald, and Wesler, has for decades helped students with disabilities obtain the kind of educational programming that helps them achieve success.

As a psychotherapist, Ms. Wesler has worked with adults, teens, and children in various settings, including both inpatient and outpatient, individual and group therapy. As a member of multiple child study teams, Ms. Wesler conducted evaluations, wrote IEPs, case managed elementary students, high-school students, and students placed in specialized, private-school programs. She also developed and facilitated various psychotherapy groups.

In her spare time, Ms. Wesler enjoys spending time with family and friends, hiking, skiing, scuba diving, snorkeling, working out, reading, traveling, and cooking.

Made in the USA
Monee, IL
10 April 2024